NICKEL-PLATED SOUL

NICKEL-PLATED SOUL

Ronald Tierney

Severn House Large Print
London & New York

This first large print edition published 2008
in Great Britain and the USA by
SEVERN HOUSE PUBLISHERS of
9-15 High Street, Sutton, Surrey, SM1 1DF.
First world regular print edition published 2004 by
Severn House Publishers, London and New York.

Copyright © 2004 by Ronald Tierney.

British Library Cataloguing in Publication Data

Tierney, Ronald
   Nickel-plated soul. - Large print ed. - (The Deets Shanahan
   mysteries)
   1. Shanahan, Deets (Fictitious character) - Fiction
   2. Private investigators - Indiana - Indianapolis - Fiction
   3. Missing persons - Investigation - Indiana - Indianapolis
   - Fiction 4. Detective and mystery stories 5. Large type
   books
   I. Title
   813.5'4[F]

   ISBN-13: 978-0-7278-7667-6

Printed and bound in Great Britain by
MPG Books Ltd, Bodmin, Cornwall.

Dedicated to Dylan Murray-Tierney

The bartender delivered the shot glass, swiped the ten-dollar bill from the bar. "Place comes to life around eleven," he said. "If you like that sort of thing."

One

The computer screen showed darkness except for the electric blue gun sights that moved through the space occupied by a maze of yellow boxes and trapezoids. Pink Floyd was on the CD player. *Meddle.* The red tank appeared from nowhere, fired. The computer emitted the sound of electronic thunder and the image on the screen shook. Apparently Howie's craft suffered a hit, but Howie's reflexes were quick. He swiveled his gun sight to the left and fired. He couldn't hear the explosion over a particularly loud section of music. But he saw the shards of light scatter in the strangely quiet destruction of his enemy.

It was a dinosaur, this game. That's why Howie could relate to it. Like him, it was a little crude, easy to understand, straightforward. The rules of this game allowed him to design his own craft, permitted him to sacrifice shields and extra ammo for speed. That was his approach to life. Travel light and move quick.

Howie, who had the blond looks and build

9

of an aging and slightly dissipated lifeguard, was thirty-nine on April 1—an auspicious date always, and now an auspicious age of which he was reminded whenever he had to fill out forms. "Are you under eighteen? Between twenty-five and thirty-eight? Or between thirty-nine and death?"

Of course this wasn't exactly true. And he knew it. There was another field, sometimes two. A large gap in the actuarial tables existed between thirty-nine and death. But he needed to feel sorry for himself and he needed an excuse for his lagging fitness.

Howie fired at the red tank that appeared between a gap as he approached the electric blue walls. Got it! He swiveled the turret and popped a series of blasts that destroyed another tank before it had a chance to get off a round. Suddenly his tank was jarred. Somewhere behind. He swiveled the sight quickly but not quickly enough. His not quite virtual tank took three more hits! *Whoop, whoop whoop!* WARNING! Howie was down to his last shield. He would blow if he didn't get the attacker. Now! *Boom!* The red tank was history.

He'd have to pick up ammo and shields before another tank appeared. If he wasn't careful, it'd all be over. Another shot. He could almost feel the shaking in his own very human, very real bones. *Boom, boom, boom.* Where was that coming from? The computer shook. Hell, the floors shook. For a moment, Howie was confused. Maybe the stereo. No. There was a muffled noise, a subtle jarring that soon separated itself from the music.

God damn it, someone was at the door! Here he was trying to stay in the game. He was about to achieve his personal best. He was trying to focus on the screen, but couldn't. He was a goner.

He wasn't expecting anyone. Only a very few dared to venture up the ragged stone steps and make the long trek back to his house. Most didn't even know it was there.

Howie went to the door, opened it. Opened it halfway. The other two guys opened it the rest of the way, pushing it in on him, pressing him back against the wall until they had entered the hall completely and had control of his body. They slammed and pushed him up the couple of steps into the small room where he had been battling aliens.

One man was pulling him up, while the other smashed an elbow into Howie's face. There were more bashes. He couldn't tell where they were coming from and he was losing track of how many assailants there were.

"You think you're getting the message?" came a question a few minutes before he blacked out.

"What message?" he asked. Then, more

desperately, after feeling another arm or fist or elbow in his face: "Tell me! What message?"

The last thing he heard before the lights went out was a moment of quiet between Pink Floyd cuts and a computer voice that said, "Sorry, game over."

Deets Shanahan's face was about four inches from the bathroom mirror. Through the lens of his drugstore glasses the seventy-year-old detective was investigating his face. Maureen had bought him the pair of tortoiseshell specs that afternoon after the wedding. It had been clear that Shanahan wasn't being obstinate by not singing the words in the hymnal. He simply couldn't see. As he inspected the face before him, the price tag dangled from the bridge of the glasses and over his nose.

"Just try them," she had told him, "you might be surprised what you can see."

He was surprised. His face was more deeply lined than he'd imagined. There were dozens of faint brown spots around his face and on his hands. He had not shaved nearly as closely or as well as he thought. He looked considerably older than he had only a moment ago. And a few wild strands of hair sprouted well past the normal confines of his eyebrows.

"I'll be damned," he said. "I'm not sure I

wanted to know all this," he said to the mirror. He turned to look at Maureen. She was a blur, a shape with auburn hair. He moved closer, looking at her as closely as he did himself. Yes, the green eyes, but they had flecks of brown. He looked at her skin, eyes glancing farther and farther downward.

"You have a lot of freckles," he said. "Much more than I realized."

"What are you doing?" she asked. "Some things aren't meant to be examined under a microscope."

Shanahan pushed the glasses down on his nose.

"Absolutely right. I look like an old man," he said.

"You *are* an old man," Maureen said. "A beautiful... lean and mean seventy-year-old man who did quite well to avoid most of the symptoms of middle age, let alone old age. No paunch..."

Shanahan's mind flashed back to this morning's wedding—Maureen's sister and her new husband—and the gaggle of fiftyish men who had fiftyish paunches and seemed almost proud of them. He had almost commented. Words from his own parents leapt to mind whenever he was on the verge of criticism.

"Until you've walked a mile in his shoes..." was one phrase of his father's. "Think your share and say nothing," was another. His

13

mother's.

On the other hand, Shanahan felt some critical stares at the reception. There he was—having passed through seven decades of existence—more than obviously attached to the bride-to-be's sister, who just happened to be young enough to be his daughter. Maureen, of course, was either oblivious to the suspect stares or, more than likely, aware but unmoved.

After nearly two years, it was still difficult for him to believe Maureen, a beautiful, spirited woman in her late forties, would want to share her life so completely with him.

"Most people have to get reading glasses by their mid-forties," Maureen continued. "You made it thirty years beyond most people."

He took them off. "I don't know."

"You don't have to wear them all the time."

"Good."

"Just when you need to see something." She laughed. "I mean when you need to read something."

He reminded himself of his good fortune.

While Maureen went out to show a prospective buyer a home somewhere in the city, Shanahan took his dog to Pleasant Run, a winding parkway that meandered around and through the East Side of Indianapolis.

Time to exercise. Both of them. Tossing the tennis ball so Casey, his sixty-pound mongrel hound, would work off some of the winter fat and so Shanahan would work some of the rust out of his own old bones.

When he came home, he fed the cat, Einstein. Flesh hung on the frame of the ancient feline like canvas on a tent pole. The cat ate more now than he did when he was younger and bigger and more muscular. But each year he became more bone. Each year he moved more slowly, cautiously, deliberately.

Shanahan opened the mail to find a number of good things: His pension check from the Army, a final check from a previous client, which he'd have to share with another detective—Howie Cross—who had helped on the case. But the best gift was the note from his grandson.

When are you coming out? I know you'll love this part of California. So will Maureen. The restaurants are wonderful around here. And San Francisco is less than an hour away. We have a great spare room with a view of the vineyard. Mother is eager to meet you as well. I've healed nicely. School is going well. Dad talks about you guys all the time. It would make him happy too.

Your grandson, Jason
P.S. Say hello to Maureen, my favorite sort of grandmother (tee hee)

15

Maureen was in the back yard—in her white blouse and khaki shorts—extending the garden farther into the lawn.

Shanahan was still looking out of the kitchen window at Maureen when the phone rang.

"Hello," Shanahan answered.

"Jish ehh ooowhee."

"What? Who is this?"

"Ooowhee."

"Who? Howie?"

"Ummm!"

"Are you drunk?"

"Noh!"

"Are you all right?"

"Noh!"

"Are you home?"

"Ummm ummm."

"I'll be right there."

If he hadn't been there several times before, Shanahan wouldn't have found the place. On a nice middle-class street with handsome older houses and nice lawns, there was a stretch of trees that leaned over the street and overgrown underbrush that inhabited the slight hill. In a narrow opening between the growth, there were stones embedded in the hill offering the adventurous a series of steps of a sort. About fifty feet from the top of steps and through a clearing was an old

16

iron gate that dangled from rusted hinges.

Beyond that was Howie Cross's house, a charming but neglected ivy-covered Mediterranean-styled chauffeur's quarters built in the 1930s. A chauffeur's quarters for what, no one knew. The location of the main house was a mystery.

"Who did this to you?" Shanahan asked, finding Howie in the bathroom, holding a wet towel to his face. Beside him was an attractive woman, wearing what appeared to be a jogging outfit. Judging by how well it all looked on her, it was clear she hadn't been doing any heavy lifting or long-distance running lately.

Howie shrugged, put the towel down. He put up two fingers, indicating two people. With still another set of hand signals, beginning to mimic a game of Charades, Cross indicated the attackers were large.

"They were bigger than a bread basket, I take it," Shanahan said.

He looked at Howie's face. Pulled out his reading glasses and examined it more closely. Christ, it was gory to see things that close. It was like seeing a flea magnified a thousand times. It is possible to see too much, he thought. The world was scary enough at a distance.

Howie's right eye was red and blue and nearly swollen shut. The nose was probably broken.

Howie smiled forlornly.

A front tooth dangled.

"God," Shanahan said. "What kind of company are you keeping these days?"

Howie shook his head. He didn't know.

"I think he should go to the hospital. He doesn't think so," the woman said. "Oh," she interrupted herself and extended her hand. "I'm Melanie."

"I'm Shanahan. I think you're right. Not about your being Melanie. About the hospital. I think we should call the police, too."

"No," Howie said.

"Why not?"

He closed his eyes, seemed to be mustering up something, maybe energy. Maybe just enough concentration to string a few sane words together.

"I'd be embarrassed."

"You been butting into somebody's business who fancies this form of reply?"

"It doesn't make any sense." Howie could talk a little better than he could over the phone, but the words were still modified by how much it hurt just to open his mouth. "They said something about 'getting the message.' Well, I didn't get it exactly. Something was lost in the translation. Ouch," he said when he touched his nose.

"Hospital time, don't you think?" Shanahan suggested. "Otherwise you'll walk around looking like Marlon Brando."

18

"What? If I don't go now, I'll gain three hundred pounds?"

"Broken nose," Melanie volunteered. "You ready to go?"

"Yeah," Howie said, giving up easily. "Better, I guess."

"What are you working on?"

"I've got one case and that can't be it."

"Mine," Melanie said.

Howie shut off the computer, looked around. He'd been given the hardest beating he'd ever had in his life and the place wasn't messed up one bit. It had all happened in a tiny space. Very controlled. The guys were professional, not just some jerks off the street. "And Shanahan, you're going to help me with my one lousy ... I don't mean lousy," he said, trying to smile at Melanie but grimacing in pain instead. "I've got one case, Shanahan."

"My lousy case," Melanie said. She smiled. "I'm kidding." She tried to kiss Howie on the cheek, but couldn't find a spot.

"You'll have to help. I can't go looking like this," Howie said.

"Where?"

"Up north. To prison."

"With me," Melanie said.

"You're the case?"

She smiled, shrugged sheepishly.

Two

Melanie drove. Her idea. The fact that she had a shiny new red Toyota Celica with all the extras and Shanahan had a 1972 Chevy Malibu with seat covers that needed seat covers might have had something to do with it. Melanie pressed some buttons on the dash and the music began. Gershwin: *American in Paris*.

Shanahan was rummaging through his mind trying to sort out the information Howie Cross had given him while they waited in the hospital and Howie tried to convince Shanahan to ride up north with Melanie—"you might get along with her father better than I would anyway."

Howie also explained what little he could piece together about his run-in. Two guys. One white for sure. The other was darker, he was sure. The only case he was working on was this one. Melanie's. Yes, he'd repossessed some cars lately and found a guy who jumped bail. But it wasn't likely that any of them would hire professional thugs for a little revenge. One car was a Camaro owned by some "redneck in Bargersville," Cross said. The other was a woman in Carmel, a prestigious area north of Indianapolis. Neither of them probably knew who, in the dark of night, repossessed their transportation.

The guy who jumped bail was a poor black kid on crack. He didn't appear to be one of the movers and shakers and the guys who stomped Cross's butt weren't from the Bloods or Crips.

"How long have you known Howie?" Shanahan asked.

"A month maybe," she said, looking forward, guiding the auto out on I-65. Her father would meet them just outside Whiting, Indiana. Not Michigan City. Not the prison. Not even that close. Six p.m. at a bar at the Three Palms Motel. Somewhere between two and three hours, depending on how she drove.

Melanie had dressed up a bit. Some make-up, a skirt; blouse and navy blazer-styled jacket. She almost looked prim. Meeting her father after thirty-five years might make a person self-conscious. Shanahan had faced a similar situation only last year. He understood.

"You remember much about him?"

The look she gave Shanahan warned that he might be treading on dangerous turf.

"No," she said.

21

"Strange," Shanahan said. "When my wife left me—way back—she took my son with her. He was ten. I didn't see him until last year. A lot of years had passed. It was tough."

"Really?" she asked warmly.

"I have a grandson I didn't even know I had."

"You were separated from your son all those years? How did that happen?"

"They moved away. I didn't try to locate her right away. Then the trail was cold. When she died, my son decided to reconnect."

"How did you feel?"

"Childish. I figured the both of them had deserted me. He was ten. I was an adult. Nothing worse than an old fool."

"Happy ending?"

"Maybe. Yes, I think so."

There was a long pause. As they left the city behind, the car passed into flat fertile farmland. Fields dotted with occasional homes and barns. Exits that led to small towns—Thorntown, Fickle and later Petit, Morocco and Roselawn. Roselawn was where the famous "Miss Nude America" was crowned once a year. In between would be Lafayette, where Purdue always boasted a bumper crop of graduating farmers and engineers, not to mention an astronaut or two.

"I don't remember them ever talking to

22

each other," Melanie said. "Dad was distant, removed. But I remember him coming in every night to give me a kiss and tuck me in. Mom ... well, I don't know what to compare her to. She was gone a lot."

"Both of them worked," Shanahan suggested.

"No, I don't think she did. She was just gone a lot. She was nice to me. I remember she spent a lot of time in front of a mirror. On one of those little benches in front of this short bureau with a big round mirror. A vanity. I picture her wearing a salmon-colored slip and smoking a cigarette. And the perfume." She shrugged. She seemed ready to leave the memories where they were.

"They ever fight?"

"No, I don't remember if they did."

"Where did your dad work?"

"Government. City, state. I don't know. It was political, that's all I know."

"What do you do, Melanie?"

"You're not usually the talkative type are you?" she asked.

"No."

"I didn't think so. Why all the questions?"

"I'm trying to make some connections."

"With what?"

"With you and with Howie's beating."

"What! You think I ... You're pretty shrewd." Her voice and her look indicated she didn't mean that in a nice way. "So, everything you've said so far was bull, right? I fell right into it. You're sharp."

"Not sharp enough or I'd have gotten a whole lot more before you figured it out."

She was silent. Angry.

"Melanie, everything I said was true."

"You think I've set up Howie or something?"

"You might not know the connection yourself. If there is any. I just don't want it to happen again. To him. Or to me. Could be connected to you or your father." He turned to look over his shoulder. There was a car behind them, but way back. Shanahan couldn't tell the make or model, which meant he wouldn't know later if it was the same car on his tail.

"You still mad?" he asked.

"Yeah." *Rhapsody in Blue* filled the silence. "You live alone?" she asked after twenty miles had passed.

"No, I live in sin." He'd never said it that way. He liked the sound of it.

Melanie laughed. "I wouldn't do anything to hurt Howie."

She'd either missed the point or was defensive about something. He didn't press it.

Whiting lies off the toll road some distance beyond Merrillville and before the Skyway exit into Chicago. The old steel mills, some deserted, some still belching smoke from skyscraping smokestacks, dominate the landscape. This is another age, another world. Mammoth, ugly steel sculptures, menacing remnants of the industrial age on the right of the toll road. On the left, three parallel sets of metal masts look more like giant alien skeletons than conduits of energy for trains into and out of Chicago.

No matter which side you looked, the world seemed tough, hard and soulless.

"Have you two corresponded? Your father and you?"

"No."

Shanahan couldn't gauge the attitude. He'd try again.

"Your going up to meet him is kind of unusual, isn't it?"

"I don't know. His being accused of killing my mother isn't exactly usual. Nothing usual about any of this, I guess. My grandmother thought someone from the family should meet him. She can't. There's no one else. I just didn't want to be alone with him right away. That's why I asked Howie to come along. Now you. Maybe I was wrong. Maybe I'm just being silly."

"I'm trying to understand a few things, that's all."

"You ever give up?"

"I'm sure I do," Shanahan said.

"My mother's body was burned in a house

25

fire. Arson, they say," Melanie said, "done by my father to make my mother's death look like an accident. This is what my grandmother told me when she thought I was old enough to understand."

"That's how she died?"

"Her skull was cracked," Melanie said, flatly.

"Why did they think your father did it?"

"He had taken out a second, very large insurance policy on her. Double indemnity clause. If she dies accidentally, it paid double. Their friends didn't help. Witnesses said they had argued a lot. About her going out. And not coming home until morning." She looked at Shanahan. "Look, I just want somebody with me, all right? How can this be connected with Howie? This was 1960. OK?"

Shanahan had been told to butt out and he knew it. There was both a pleading and a threat in her "OK?" that suggested she wanted to be friendly but not necessarily friends.

It was twilight time at the Palms Motel when they pulled into the bumpy parking lot. Fresh tufts of grass grew in the cracks of the concrete. There was a fifteen-year-old Cadillac parked in front of one of the rooms. The only other car in the lot was parked off to one side of the office. The bar was across

26

the drive. A couple of neon palm fronds stuttered at the approaching darkness.

Miami? Havana? Right there in the shadow of the northern Indiana steel mills it was, having survived another cold gray winter.

"Looks like the party was over a long time ago," Shanahan said.

If the outside wasn't convincing, the inside wasn't exactly swinging to a Latin beat. No sparkling lights. No Xavier Cugat.

A bald guy, his back to the bar, was intent on something in the cash drawer. The only other person was a small man in the corner. The place was dark. The man's face looked red and evil, lit by a candle stuck in a red glass. The flame was gasping.

"Is that him?"

"I don't know," she said. The guy motioned.

"I can wait at the bar," Shanahan said. She didn't argue.

"Miller," Shanahan said.

"Lite, Genuine Draft, Genuine Draft Lite, Lite Ice?"

"The real one. And a shot of D.W. Dant." He could handle it. He was just along for the ride. She was driving. He was depressed. He remembered the time this place was stuck in.

He looked over at the reconciliation. They didn't look all that happy to see each other. His eyes retreated back over the dirty, thick-pile carpet that soaked up all the sounds of their conversation.

Melanie's dad snapped his fingers. The bartender put a bottle and a glass in front of Shanahan and went over to the table. He came back, pouring rum and something clear into a glass. He hustled over to the table. Came back.

"Bet you can handle the crowd," Shanahan said. Maybe Melanie's father chose this place for a reason. Maybe because it was quiet. Maybe it was a favorite old haunt. Maybe he had met someone else there earlier. After all, he had to get from Michigan City to Whiting somehow. And he did all this traveling for a reason. Maybe the bartender knew what it was.

The bartender delivered the shot glass, swiped the ten-dollar bill from the bar. "Place comes to life around eleven," he said. "If you like that sort of thing."

"What?"

"Life."

"Oh that," Shanahan said, looked back over to the table. "You know the guy?"

"Nope."

"He come in alone?"

"What is this?"

"Family reunion," Shanahan said. "Know anything?"

"Pierre is the capital of South Dakota and Millard Fillmore was the thirteenth president of these here United States." He plopped change from the ten down on the bar.

"Nobody's talking to me today," Shanahan said.

"Talk. I got talk. I just don't have answers. My mama used to say 'ask me no questions and I'll tell you no lies.' What do you think of the Bears?"

"I don't."

"The Bulls?"

"Nothing."

"Well, we tried, didn't we?" the bartender said, moving down the bar to cut some orange wedges, which he decorated with maraschino cherries.

"The Cubs?" Shanahan volunteered.

"Pfft," the bartender said. "The June Taylor Dancers are better than the Cubs. The Sox?"

"Designated hitter," Shanahan said, letting the bartender know his thoughts on the American League.

That was that.

"He wants to meet you," Melanie said. He hadn't heard her coming. "He said to come over to the table. He'll buy you a drink." She raised her eyebrows and shrugged. She didn't understand whatever had gone on during their meeting.

"You OK?" Shanahan asked her.

"Yeah, fine. I just don't know what I'm doing here. I'm going to the powder room," she said with the disdain of a woman reminded of her womanhood and its "proper" place in the scheme of things.

The guy didn't get up. It was hard to tell much in the dim light, but the man looked pale, drawn. His eyes held no life. But there was nothing threatening about him. Chances were no one would pick him out as an ex-convict. Chances were that no one would pick him out of the crowd at all. If there were a couple more human beings in the Three Palms Lounge, Melanie's father would be invisible. In front of him was an ashtray with several non-filtered cigarette butts crushed into the ashes.

"Nice ride up here?" the guy asked.

"Long."

"Yeah." He looked around. "I like this place. It's like picking up where I left off. Outside, it's pretty strange. Cars are different. Christ." He shook his head. "Prices. Buck twenty-five for a good glass of liquor in a nice place. You remember that? Now? Hell, you have to cash in a bearer bond to get a glass of Scotch. It'll all be strange for awhile."

"It'll come pretty quick," Shanahan suggested.

"Maybe. I did thirty-five years for killing my wife. Every day of it. No parole. Paid the

30

full price. Didn't watch much TV. Didn't read newspapers or magazines. I wanted it that way, you know. Simple. I couldn't afford to take on any new stuff, you know. Keep focused. Didn't want to crowd out what happened. I just had one brief glimpse of what it's like out there—from Michigan City to Whiting. Different world now. No doubt I'm in for a few more surprises. Thought about changing my name to Winkle." The guy waited for a response. Didn't get any. He looked at Shanahan. "You know, I like a guy without a sense of humor."

Shanahan smiled.

"Look," the guy said. "I need a guide for awhile. I'm not gonna hang that on Melanie. You interested?"

"No, I'm not."

"She says you're a private investigator. I just want to hire you for a job. It's simple."

"What you need is a tour guide."

"Afraid I can't pay you? I can."

"Don't take offense. It's not my line of work."

"Listen, I've got some investigation to do. It's a job. A real job. I need a guy who can help me find somebody."

"Who?"

"My wife."

"The dead one?"

"You got it."

31

Three

There were dozens of reasons Shanahan was attracted to Maureen. The obvious one was he found her beautiful. But there was also emotional warmth. There was a cheerfulness, optimism, she possessed that made the light shine a little brighter when she was in the room. She was open, honest, fair. She also passionately enjoyed life and was more than willing to drag him kicking and screaming back into the world of the living.

These were the thoughts he had climbing into bed next to her, gathering in her scented warmth. Two things had triggered the thoughts, he supposed. The bartender's little quip about "life, if you like that sort of thing," and Melanie's father, Hugh Dart. Dart spent thirty-five years removed in many ways from the passage of time. So had Shanahan before she came into his life. In this very house, decades after his wife and son had left him, he had allowed time to slip away, unused for the most part, a blandness punctuated by an occasional case and a few nights with Harry at the bar.

Maureen changed all that. Full of life. Very full. Of course, you couldn't prove it now. Her body had finally given up for the day, though reluctantly, it seemed. The television was still on—night-light, now, for Shanahan to undress and slip into bed. The bluish light of the David Letterman show flickered on the wall and on the white sheets. Shanahan reached across her to get the remote.

"You hungry?" she asked, barely audible.

"No," he said. He was, but he was too tired to eat.

"Pizza," she said, still groggy. "Greek. From Bazbeaux's. I can warm it up."

"It's all right." Shanahan pushed the button. The room went dark. He meant to kiss her on the neck—a good-night kiss.

She turned and in the dark his lips landed somewhere around her nose.

Maureen laughed. "Too late."

"What?"

"I'm awake. How'd it go?"

"Who knows?"

"Surely you do."

"A guy is getting out of prison for killing his wife. I go up with his daughter, who doesn't want to go alone. He acts like he could care less about his daughter. Instead, he asks me to help him find his wife."

"Her grave?"

"No."

"Is he crazy?"

"Who knows?" He kissed her. This time he found her lips.

"Good work," she said. "The kiss, I mean. A little whiskey, eh?"

"To sleep. Einstein talked me into it."

"That cat. A bad influence."

"Yes. When I came in, I let Casey out for his usual inspection of the perimeter and Einstein nagged me into the kitchen. I was afraid he'd wake you, so I gave in. He kind of nudged the whiskey bottle."

"So you two had a drink?"

"I thought it was a good idea. He's devious. Gets me all liquored up, talks me into the whole jar of cat snacks."

"So did you take the job? A little jaunt into the spirit world might be interesting."

"I told him I was just standing in for Howie Cross and that he should talk to Howie. I think that made the daughter happy and that will make Howie happy. And everybody lived happily ever after," Shanahan said, punctuating "the end," with what he expected to be a final kiss before drifting off. Certainly he was tired enough.

"Except for the wife," Maureen said, her voice anticipating her brain's soft drop into sleep.

Hugh Dart kept him awake. Most of God's creatures had some passion that kept them going. For his dog it was as simple as a tennis ball. For Einstein it was food. No one was ever in the kitchen alone. For Maureen, it was the unlimited opportunity for discovery. Or Häagen-Dazs Swiss Almond Vanilla.

For Shanahan, it had always been the sense of something left undone. Perhaps an iota of curiosity. Now, it was Maureen that made getting out of bed each morning something less than a chore. For Hugh Dart, it appeared that finding his wife—who was, by all accounts, dead, buried and presumably easily accounted for—was the reason to keep on living.

"What did you do all that time in prison, Hugh?" Shanahan had asked him on the long and largely quiet three hours back to Indianapolis.

"Served my time," he said, "remembering everything I ever heard her say."

Morning didn't take the edge off Shanahan's uneasiness. At dawn he quietly fed and nursed his charges—one tiny white pill for the hyperthyroid cat and one pellet-shaped buffered aspirin for his arthritic dog. Sour faces on both as they dutifully took their respective doses. All the while he tried to make sense of the bizarre request from Hugh Dart and the seemingly senseless beating of Howard Cross.

Maureen was still in bed. She was usually first in at night and last out in the morning, getting her usual eight hours while Shanahan had slowly been drawn down to six. He put a towel over the coffee grinder to muffle the sound. Still it whirred, finally giving up a pot's worth of brown dust. The cat teetered off the counter to a chair, then to the floor, where his teetering turned into tottering, his bony body making an unsteady journey to the litter box.

Einstein had made it to spring. There had been some doubt. So, too, the aged apple tree, losing limbs to hard freezes and ice storms. The roots managed to feed a few branches and sparse and puny buds. Einstein and the tree were marks to measure accomplishments against the odds, reminders that all things are temporary.

The newspaper held no surprises. In fact the usualness of the news was a relentless lulling, a Pavlovian seduction, despite the fullness in caffeine in Maureen's favorite "Viennese Blend." He fought nodding off. At the third or fourth nod—who's counting?—he forced himself from the chair. He would get some gas and head over to Howie's neighborhood. He would canvass the neighbors. Had anyone seen anything? The thugs? The car?

He hated this part. Asking inane questions of strangers, interrupting their morning patterns—most of them timing to the minute where they had to be at any given moment to be on time for work. Yet, he needed to do it now. He needed to be there before they all left for their offices, stores and factories.

The day was beautiful. Howie's neighborhood looked a little like a park. Trees. Lots of trees—big old oaks and maples, slightly beyond bud stage and smaller white dogwoods, flowering crabs, feathery pink buds. The light was soft, the air barely cool. Spring was evident and almost offset the drudgery and misery of the long brutal winters.

The neighbors to the right and left of Howie's little hideaway were polite but not helpful. Why should they be? This was the North Side. Some people would call North Side residents unfriendly. Others would say they merely minded their own business. Either way, no one had noticed anything unusual yesterday.

Shanahan stopped a young man in a baseball cap coming out of a house directly across from Howie's. The young man seemed intent on weeding a flowerbed. Had he seen anything unusual? "No." Strangers? "No." Shrugged shoulders. Not unfriendly, but not encouraging. Unusual cars?

"Yeah," he said. "A white something or other. Didn't see who drove it."

"Why do you remember it?"

"It's where I usually park," he said.

"Anything unusual about the car?"

"No. Had Illinois plates. That's not strange, is it?"

"It'll do," Shanahan said.

The time was right if the guy was right about the car. Only there a short time, he remembered. Large car. Blue interior. "Kind of fancy."

"I appreciate your help."

"Are you a cop?" He pulled up his baseball cap. The look was puzzled. The tone was disbelieving, even before Shanahan answered, as though the questioner asked the question despite the fact that the answer was obvious.

"Do you always look this ugly?" Shanahan asked Howie Cross, who answered the door wearing a blanket.

"Only after I've been beaten to a pulp or when I have to get up this early in the morning. It is a rare thing for you to have witnessed both. You know the vampires have not even gotten to sleep yet?"

"There's a guy out there weeding his flower bed," Shanahan said.

"Where's my gun?"

Shanahan followed Cross back inside, witnessed him as he gently, delicately closed the door to the bedroom. He came back into the living room, rearranging his blanket in an act of modesty.

38

"So, you know anybody from Chicago who means you harm?"

"What makes you ask that?" Cross asked, moving toward the kitchen. Pans rattled.

"Car outside while you were being manhandled had Illinois plates."

"Illinois is a big state."

"Not really," Shanahan said. "Not likely these guys were from Springfield."

"East St. Louis," Cross shouted. "Tough town. I'm sure even Peoria has a few ruffians. Ruffians? I don't think I've ever used that word before. You think they were ruffians?"

"You do something bad to someone from East St. Louis?"

"Don't know anybody from East St. Louis. But just didn't want you dismissing the entire state of Illinois out of hand."

There was a long silence while Howie was presumably making coffee. "OK," he said, "OK. Chicago. But it makes no more sense than East St. Louis." Howie sat on the sofa, rearranged his blanket. "I do have another question."

"Shoot."

"Who's paying for your time and why?" Howie was speaking better. They'd even screwed his tooth back in.

"I hadn't thought about it. Maybe I just didn't like the idea of someone coming over here and beating you up?"

"That's sweet, Shanahan," Howie said.

"And not knowing why."

"So you know why now?"

"No. But I could speculate."

"Speculate while I pour the coffee. Black, right?"

"Yes." Shanahan followed. "Why would Hugh Dart get out of prison at Michigan City and go all the way over to Whiting to be picked up? And why is your kitchen so neat?"

"Mr. Hugh Dart had no explanation for his diversion?"

"No. And Whiting is a stone's throw from Chicago."

"And the car that carried the thugs who beat me to a pulp had Illinois plates."

"Of course they could be from Springfield," Shanahan teased.

He followed the blanket-draped Howie Cross back into the living room. Watching the groggy P.I. trying to hold onto his coffee and still keep his body wrapped. He sat on the sofa.

"Or East St. Louis," Shanahan continued.

"Your point is that Melanie's father is somehow involved." He took a sip, cursed. "Dammit, the ... I swore I'd never have a microwave. Just what I need. Third-degree burns on the parts of my lip that aren't already scabs."

"Just connected is all I'm saying."

40

The door opened slowly and Melanie came out into the room, a sheet wrapped around her body.

"What are you guys?" Shanahan asked. "Bedouins?"

Four

"Harry, what are you doin'?" Shanahan asked.

"Mildewin'," Harry said, opening up a roll of nickels and letting them drop into the drawer of the cash register. It was nearly ten in the morning. No one was likely to show up at Harry's bar until eleven.

"What were you doing about this time in 1960?"

Harry, a small man with silver hair who favored forties actor Barry Fitzgerald, thought a moment, slammed the stubborn roll of dimes against the edge of the register.

"Here probably."

"Right here at this very bar, is that what you're saying?"

"Listen, you think you're cute, but it could've been right here. You and I have spent a lot of time right here in this very place, back when this used to be Delaney's. Probably on that very stool."

"Not at this hour," Shanahan said.

The shutters were open and the spring light invaded the place. Like most bars, it didn't fare well under natural light. The place looked clean but a little tattered. The glossy reproduction of a reclining Rubenesque nude lost its night-time sensuous humor. It struck Shanahan as very cheap and slightly grotesque.

"I was out of the Army by then. Driving a taxi," Harry continued.

"We were here in Indianapolis?"

"Yep. I'd separated from the Army in late '58. Your first wife—what's her name?"

"I only had one, Harry. That was Elaine."

"Well I count Maureen, whether it's all legal or not," Harry said. "Elaine introduced me to my third wife, remember. You came back to stand up with me."

"Whatever possessed me to do that?" Shanahan asked rhetorically. Shanahan couldn't remember the sixties. Rather, decades were blurred. Long-term memory loss, this one was. But it was about the time Elaine took off with his son and Shanahan entered a thirty-year deep freeze. Aside from a few beers, Cubs games and a hand or two of euchre, Shanahan had become pretty disengaged with the world. Shanahan's review reinforced his notion that Hugh Dart had nothing on him.

"It was a tradition, you being my best man at my weddings," Harry said.

"One that will no doubt continue. You ever hear of Hugh Dart?"

"Nope."

"I thought you knew all the murderers, movie stars, sports heroes and kings and queens. And you tell me you don't know Hugh Dart?"

Harry prided himself on keeping up with the important people. Important people for Harry ranged from Tiny Tim, who tiptoed through the tulips, to Jonas Salk, who picked up a Nobel Prize. It was a good trait for a bartender, as was Harry's story-telling. And all of these talents tended to override Harry's tendency to boss everyone around, including the clientele. He wouldn't hesitate a moment to tell them what was good for them and what wasn't. Yet Harry, despite this drawback and the incredibly bad stew he inflicted on the unwary, had actually built up the business from the old Delaney days.

"And which category might this Hugh Dart fall into here?" Harry said, a mild disgust seeping into his voice.

"Murderer. Murdered his wife, they say. Burned down the house to make it look like an accident."

"Murder and embezzlement. Two million dollars never accounted for. Dammit! I remember that. How'd I forget it? I'm getting to be more like you every day."

"Tell me about the money."

"Never got him on that. Never could prove it. Just the murder. Course that's enough in most cases. They almost fried him on that one. Why are you asking?"

"If I had some coffee, I'd probably feel more in the mood to talk."

"You use this place like a library, like it's your personal office and now I'm expected to supply the coffee. I'm out of coffee." Harry's anger was easily ignited and quickly extinguished. It rarely lasted more than a few seconds.

"I smell it, Harry." Shanahan knew he'd get his cup of coffee. News of any scandal was impossible for his old pal to resist. "I get coffee, you get news."

"It's blackmail, Deets."

"You were holdin' out."

"How do you know him?" Melanie asked. She was in the bathroom, in front of the mirror, trying to get her hair right. Cross was behind her.

"Shanahan? We did a couple of cases together."

"You like him?"

"Yes, I do."

"Why?"

"Straight shooter. You don't like him?"

"I don't know. He's nosy."

"That's what we do for a living, Melanie."

"You're not nosy."

"I'm not nosy enough," he said, putting his hands on her waist. "Let's see ... Ummm ...

45

what were you like at eighteen?"

She laughed. "I was shallow. Like now. I was very concerned about how I looked, what other people thought about me—which I thought depended entirely on what I wore. Let's see. Believe it or not, I hadn't had sex."

"Were you as beautiful then as you are now?"

"No," she said with mock seriousness. "I have gotten more beautiful each year. By the time I'm ninety, people will be falling at my feet, I'll be so spectacularly beautiful. My turn, have you always been so glib and transparent?"

"Always. Like you, though not only shallow, but glib as well. Complementary traits. We make a nice couple, don't you think?"

"So far so good."

But you're not really telling me much, are you?"

"What do you mean? What are you looking for?"

"Well, you had a mother who was murdered and a father in prison for doing it. Hard to imagine you were all that shallow, running by babbling brooks and singing happy little songs."

She turned from the mirror. "That was a long time ago. I've gotten on with my life. I'm more interested in the future. Now," she said, pausing for a moment and moving out of the bathroom and away from him, "how much do you want to be part of it?"

It was a little before noon when Shanahan got home. The temperature had hit 60, a pleasant sunny 60 degrees. After the worst winter in decades, 60 was a scorcher.

Maureen was in the back garden, in gray sweats. The wheelbarrow beside her held mounds of dirt. Sprouting from them were fern fronds.

"The ferns were getting too thick out front. I thought I'd bring some back here," she said as Shanahan approached. Casey ran to her side, sat obediently and some might say admiringly. Casey had fallen in love with Maureen immediately. Then again, cautious of men and ferocious toward strange men, the spotted and speckled hound would have allowed any woman to steal his food and burgle the home. "I need to expand the garden a little."

"I know, but Casey's not exactly sensitive about the fauna and flora, especially when it keeps making the lawn smaller."

She sighed, blowing air out of her lips. "He's getting older. He doesn't want to run around so much."

"The yard is shrinking faster than the dog is getting older. He needs to run a little."

She smiled. "I'll give them to my sister."

"I don't mean to be so bossy."

"You're not." She kissed him on the cheek. "I wasn't thinking. Where've you been?"

"To see Cross, and I dropped by Harry's."

"What's up?"

Shanahan related Harry's sketchy memories of Hugh Dart and the city's "trial of the decade." Hugh Dart was the director of a huge state agency. Had a lot of say-so about who got what contracts. He was young, prominent in political circles, but while the wife enjoyed the increasing celebrity, she was impatient with the extremely slow growth of his income. State officials get very little from the taxpayers. Directly. Dart's wife had him scurrying just to pay for her Ayres charge account and her even more expensive trips to Marshall Fields in Chicago.

"Marriage was heading for ruin," Shanahan said. "Hugh Dart takes out $100,000 policy on his wife. No sooner had it taken effect than she is found dead inside her burned abode. Insurance on her and the house. Double indemnity on her because it was an accident, or so it seemed initially. Autopsy shows head received a severe blow. Deadly force, they say."

"Why would someone risk all that for $100,000? I mean it's a lot of money, more in 1960. But..."

"Why would he risk murder unless he could live the rest of his life in luxury?"

"Maybe it wasn't a matter of wanting the

48

money but of having to have it?" Maureen made a good point, Shanahan thought, but Maureen continued. "Even so, how dumb would he have to be to do it after buying a new insurance policy? Men weren't insuring their wives then anyway."

"Desperate men do desperate things," Shanahan said. "Harry remembers there were some unaccounted for funds. Rumors of embezzlement—kickbacks to Dart. Harry wasn't sure how much but it was as he put it, 'big money.'"

"If it was so much," Maureen said slowly, contemplating, seemingly reconsidering Dart's intelligence, if not his morals. "All the more reason not to have taken out an insurance policy."

"I'm not sure how bright the man is."

"I want to talk to you," Hugh Dart said over the phone.

"What do we have to talk about?" Shanahan said.

"Let's just meet, have a little chat. I'll buy you dinner tomorrow. OK?"

Curiosity got the best of Shanahan. He didn't much care about Hugh Dart or about finding the wife, if in fact she was more than a set of burnt ivory in a box six feet under. But it still bugged him that someone stopped by Howie's house and did some unlicensed dental work.

49

"I know a bar on Tenth ... a friend..."

"Listen. I want to buy you a really good dinner. St. Elmo's. Brings back memories."

"Sure you want to?"

"You bet I do. And hell, that's the only thing that's the same down here. I'm at Circle Center now. The mall ... like Jupiter or something. Spent all day here. You know virtual reality?"

"I'm still working on this one. What time?"

"Seven. St. Elmo's." Hugh Dart laughed.

Five

"Why?" asked Lieutenant Max Rafferty, Indianapolis Police Department. Public Affairs.

"Because I'm curious," Shanahan said. He was pacing with the phone. The dog paced with him. He'd asked for Lieutenant Swann, and after several clicks and tones was transferred to Rafferty. The last person he wanted to talk to was Rafferty. No love lost. A lot of malice existed. But closed cases had to go through Rafferty. And as decent as Swann was, he played everything by the book. Not so Rafferty.

"That's not good enough," Rafferty said after Shanahan made his request.

"Private citizen. Freedom of information."

"Closed case, Shanahan."

"I know. You guys occasionally get a homicide conviction. At least you used to."

"Who was it?"

"Hugh Dart, convicted of killing his wife, Barbara."

"I'm not familiar with it," Rafferty said.

"I'd be surprised if you were. It was 1960.

51

I know you don't have enough toes and fingers for this one, but chances are you were chasing Cherry Vodka with some Schlitz malt liquor at a drive-in somewhere, wishing you had a girl. Or maybe you were working over at the Tee Pee making a Wimpy Burger."

"Good, Shanahan. You're getting much better at these lines." He laughed. "Actually you're not far off. Probably hanging out at Al Green's. A greasy tenderloin and load of French-fried onion rings, watching that dinky screen and terrible movies he had out there. C'mon, Shanahan, what do you need? I'm not a bad guy and since you're an old man and probably gonna die soon, I don't mind helping you out one little bit."

"Helluva guy, Rafferty. Hugh Dart."

"You said that."

"Convicted in 1960 of killing his wife, burning down the house and maybe some embezzlement thrown in." If he'd been able to talk with Swann, maybe he would have brought up the rough and tumble at Howie's place. But Rafferty disliked Cross even more than he did Shanahan. And letting the police know was really Howie's call anyway. Maybe Howie knew more than he was saying. Could have been particularly nasty bill collectors.

"What do you want to know?"

"Everything."

"Figures."

There were no goodbyes.

That was all Shanahan was going to do tonight. Dinner, watch the Chicago game. The season was in its infancy. The Cubs still had a chance.

Tomorrow he'd look back in time. He wanted to see what the newspapers had to say about Hugh Dart.

Central Library, on St. Clair, between Meridian and Pennsylvania, is one of the few grand old buildings not torn down during various visionless mayoralties. It had been handsomely restored.

Shanahan was guided up one of the grand staircases to a hall that led into one of the new wings, then toward an elevator that stopped on a cold, windowless room that contained an assortment of microfilm viewers.

He took out the films that covered January 1960 to September 1960 from the drawers that contained the pages of the *Indianapolis Star* and the now defunct *Indianapolis Times*. Some instruction followed. Soon newsprint glided dizzily across the screen, chronicling the days after Fabian and before the Rolling Stones.

It came back quickly. Eisenhower was president. It would be the last year for the smiling grandfatherly Ike, who was, Shanahan learned from military gossip, as mean as a snake when not in public. Nixon had a cakewalk for the Republican nomination, though Nelson Rockefeller carried a barrel of banana peels. A young upstart named Kennedy was challenging popular Hubert Humphrey and treacherous Lyndon Johnson for the Democratic nomination.

Nothing in the first few issues of January. No Dart. He had noticed names of places long gone. Movie theaters like Keith's, Loews and the Lyric were gone from the downtown, though the Indiana was converted to a repertory theater and the Circle was home to the Symphony. Neighborhood theaters were all gone. There were names he'd forgotten. The Garfield, Hamilton, Belmont, Pixy and Old Trail.

Downtown department stores like Wasson's and the William H. Block & Co. were gone from the city, from the earth. L.S. Ayres had changed owners more times than a TV network and left downtown for the suburbs. Ads flashed before him. He imagined how Hugh Dart must feel. Where were the familiar restaurants? St. Elmo's might be it. Who else was left? Where was the Key West Shrimp House? Where was the King Cole? And Sam's Subway with the beautiful hostess and the best martini olives in the city?

When the doors clanged shut on Hugh

Dart in Michigan City, things began to disappear.

Cars were different too. In 1960, you could still buy a DeSoto or Studebaker or a Nash Rambler or a Corvair. The foreign makes that invaded in the sixties were long gone. But in 1960, according to the ads, you could buy a Renault Dauphine for $1645, a Morris for $1495, a Hillman for $1795. Fiats were being sold in the states, as were Triumphs, MGs and Vauxhalls. When was the last time he'd even seen a Morris or a Hillman on the road?

Shanahan pushed forward. He was being sucked in not so much by how things were as by how many things were missing. Gone. *Pfft.* A puff of smoke.

A few issues later, there it was. Hugh Dart, State Budget Director, arrested. The *Times* had a photo. A handsome, stylish Hugh Dart was sandwiched between a uniformed cop and, according to the caption, John G. Radiquet, Dart's attorney. The headline read: "Grand Jury indicts state official." The subhead was: "Wife slain, burned."

Barbara Dart, the story said, had been killed a month earlier at 9:30 in the evening. Her head had not been cracked open as Melanie had said. There was a bullet lodged in the brain—.38. Arson inspectors verified that the house had been set on fire intentionally. That's all that anyone would say formally. The trial was set for June.

The next day's paper quoted Dart saying he was innocent. According to the story, the alleged murderer could not account for his time and chose not to answer the reporters' other questions. There was no mention of embezzlement.

However, there had been a running story on the State Teacher's Retirement Fund. Federal officials were being called in to investigate. Governor Handley was not happy about the whole thing. There was also a story on the sentencing of one Virgil "Red" Smith. Highway scandals during a previous Governor's watch. Same party. Didn't look good for the Republicans.

According to the story, Virgil had been convicted of accepting $7793 in bribes from someone selling thirty-six power shovels, whatever those were. The sentence, two to fourteen years. Seven thousand dollars, hardly in the league of Hugh Dart's possible two million dollar scam. Then again, there was more to state budgets than highways.

The strobe-like effect of the news pages flashing by as he attempted to see through his new drugstore glasses made Shanahan a little nauseous and he was working his way up to a headache. But he pressed forward. Through stories on Cuba, the upcoming election, more stories on the Teacher's Retirement Fund. No mention of Vietnam though it had actually begun to fester by then. Elvis got out of the Army without his sideburns. Arnold Palmer was a national hero. Even as a reluctant Hoosier, Shanahan remembered the glowing reports of Indiana-born Oscar Robertson's success at the University of Cincinnati, a foreshadowing of his pro days.

Later, on September 2 the temperature was 93 degrees at the State Fair, the Cubs were twenty-six games out of first place and Hugh Dart was convicted of killing his wife. Still no mention of embezzlement or bribery related to the condemned man. Two weeks later, he was sentenced to thirty-five to fifty years in prison.

He was lucky, an editorial said. Many of Indiana's murderers were being fried in Indiana's electric chair. After all, there was proof of "cold-blooded premeditation."

"I don't take any cases," John G. Radiquet said to Shanahan inside a small, handsome office in Circle Tower. "I just come in here to get away from the wife and have a good smoke or three." He smiled, dabbed the burning end of his cigar against the glass ashtray.

Shanahan guessed him to be in his seventies. About right. From the photo in the *Times*, he looked to be a little older than his client. Now he was a little heavy, wore a tan

57

and sported a sparse head of silver hair, dutifully combed as if there were more. There was no pretense. It was merely combed in the style he had had for forty years.

"You stay in contact with Hugh Dart?" Shanahan asked.

"Hugh was a strange one," Radiquet said, shaking his head. "Almost had me convinced he was innocent. Not by any evidence, you understand. Just the way he talked. When he was convicted, there were a couple of things in the proceedings that might have gotten us an appeal. He'd have none of it. I expected to hear from him when he came up for parole. Nothing. He's out, I take it?"

"Yes. He's asked me to find his wife."

Radiquet almost laughed. His body shook in silent, ironic amusement. He smiled, raised his eyebrows, shook his head again and shrugged.

"This world and the next," he said. "Funny thing, he did seem shocked by her death in the beginning. That's the way I saw it, anyway. Then he got real cool. And he said, that's not her. And he got real calm. Real distant. I tried to talk to him. He was polite, cooperative but as cold as tits on a brass monkey in January." Radiquet chewed on his cigar.

"Could he have been right?"

"Hard to imagine. There were no dental records to make comparisons. No DNA like today. She was a she. She was the right height, right bone structure. Diamond that matched the one on her engagement ring was found on her bones in the ashes. Right cut, right karat. And hell, the right place at the right time. I think the guy went a little wacky. Wanna know my pet theory?"

"Yes, I do," Shanahan said.

"I think he loved her. Then in a jealous rage, he killed her. He realized how much he loved her and, not so much to prove his innocence as to believe she's still alive, he's blocked out ever having done the crime in the first place."

Made sense to Shanahan. He looked out the window, onto the street below, across the brick street that circled around the Soldier's and Sailor's monument. He saw what used to be the Hilton, then the Ramada and now the Radisson Hotel. He thought it had been a Holiday Inn for awhile. The building never changed. Only the names changed. Something funny going on there, he thought. He turned back to the attorney. Radiquet's insanity theory made sense. Still Shanahan wondered how the insurance policy figured into it.

"He's done his time," Radiquet continued. "My guess is that he will occupy most of his time hunting the ghost of his wife. Strange mission. But it's something to do."

"What about the insurance policy? That

makes it sound like premeditation."

"Sure, that's exactly the conclusion the jury came to, I'd bet my life on it. That's what did him in. Frankly, that's the weird part. A guy as smart as Hugh Dart—and the man was brilliant—would never have taken out an insurance policy before a murder. The guy probably did it; but was he convicted on the wrong evidence."

"You say he was brilliant."

"Absolutely. Political strategist. Big-time Republican. Used to see him down at the Columbia Club. Lunch everyday with one bigwig or another. Out of my league even, and I was no slouch in those days. Talk to Daniel Block. Used to be a reporter for the *Times*. Knows about these things."

"I appreciate it, Mr. Radiquet. I'm amazed you remember it all so clearly. I can't remember what happened that long ago." Shanahan started toward the door.

"Don't be in such a hurry. Cigar?"

"No thanks."

"My biggest case. Hell to lose it. But I did all right. He wasn't executed. Everybody viewed that as some sort of miracle on my part. It wasn't. In the end, the publicity was responsible for getting me a lot of work." Radiquet nodded toward the window. "You remember the English Hotel?"

"No, should I?"

"Figured you were old enough. Used to be

60

down there on the Circle. Had balconies overlooking the city. Great. Busy town then. Everything was buzzing. Streetcars. A few horses even."

"Not in 1960."

"No, no," he said, laughing. A laugh that turned into a cough. When he recovered, he continued. "No, earlier. Just reminiscing, sir. Hell, they tore down the Claypool too. Now they have some modern hotel and a betting parlor. Dad would have liked that part of it. I remember seeing my dad in the old Claypool when he got older. Retired. Sitting there with his cronies, enjoying a cigar, talking about the days that were. No lobby to go to these days to just sit and smoke and talk. Great places downtown, then. The characters over there in the City Market. The Fox burlesque house. Got pretty shady toward the end. I remember playing pool in the Board of Trade Building. Downstairs. Some serious games. Some toughs. Gone too."

Shanahan realized the guy wanted to talk. Had nothing else to do.

"I wasn't here then. Not all that much, anyway. In the Army, somewhere. Don't know a whole lot about the city before the sixties."

"Used to be the inter-urban. Went up to Broad Ripple. Talk about a place. What a place that was. In the summer. It was like a

61

regular resort community. Now, what is it? Lot of bars, lot of rock 'n' roll. Nothing like it was."

"Nothing is much like it used to be," Shanahan said.

"That's not the problem. The worse thing is, nothing is ever like you thought it was gonna be," the man said, laying his cigar in the ashtray and turning away for a moment to his bookshelves. Lines of leather-bound books. His leather chair creaked. He hovered a few moments over a book and Shanahan didn't know whether to leave or not. "When you're young, history is for old people, the future is golden. When you're old, the future is bleak, but the past was golden. Anywhere but here and now, right?" He laughed. "That's my theory of mid-life crisis, you know. When you have to turn around like that—finally figuring out where you're supposed to look—forward or backward. That moment's a killer."

The air was filled with the smell of tobacco and leather. There was another scent that was familiar. He noticed a shelf with a sliding door. The door was partially open. He could make out the label of a bottle of port.

"There," Radiquet said, swiveling back around and putting the book down flat on the desk. He opened what appeared to be a ledger; but it was actually newspaper clippings, yellowed clippings secured by yellowed tape. "There she is. There she ... was."

Barbara Dart was blonde, hair up like Lana Turner. Lipsticked smile. Heavy eyelashes. Barbara Dart, Hugh, Radiquet, his wife, two other men and two other women were seated at a table.

"Who are the others?"

"Doctor...uh, dammit. What! Doctor uh. Doctor Pritchardt." He nodded as the rest of the name came to him. "Augustus Pritchardt. State hospitals. They were his. Don't remember her name. She's dead now."

"And him?"

"Hanging on. See him at the Club. We lost touch, he and I. The other man is Samuel Dickerson. Auto dealer, campaign contributor. Shame how I remember his name. We used to kid him. He had these big picture windows down there on Keystone Avenue and he'd have 'bring your wife' written on the window. Big letters. And we used to tell him he should say 'bring your wife and let's dick her, son.'"

Shanahan didn't laugh.

Radiquet shrugged, looked back down at the photograph. "Key West Shrimp House. The Darts were regulars. She liked the little umbrellas in the drinks."

The guys had martinis. She was holding a cigarette and you could see the lipstick print on the end.

"So, you knew her?"

"We were friends with Hugh. Helen, my wife, and I were friends with Barbara as we had been with Hugh's first wife."

"Barbara was his second?" Shanahan felt like someone getting a spritzer in the face.

"Yeah, mini-scandal," Radiquet said, picking up his cigar. "Barbara jumped out of a cake in New York." He noticed the not-quite-believing look on Shanahan's face. "True," he nodded. "Didn't make as big a difference as it might. Hugh wasn't ever going to run for office. Hugh was content to run the person who got elected. The power behind and all that. The only people who knew his name were the ones who counted. Behind the scenes. That's all he was interested in. He was young, but right before he was arrested, he was immensely influential. Kingmaker eventually, I'm sure. Strategist, for damn sure. He knew. He knew how hard he could push. He had everybody's number but his new wife's. She was a looker. She was a schemer. Maybe better than he was."

"And the kid, Melanie?"

"First wife's."

"Why was she with Barbara?"

"First one was institutionalized. Couldn't handle the divorce. Never was the same. Here's another," Radiquet said turning a couple of pages. "This is Hugh and me. That's the Governor. Columbia Club. About

64

a year before Hugh was convicted."

"That simple. Dart just dumped his wife for Barbara?"

"Most men would have. Hugh had married young. Sweet woman. But no intellectual competitor for Hugh. Wanted him home evenings by the fire. Wanted kids. Probably wanted Hugh to become a scoutmaster or president of the PTA. Hell, she wanted him to become Fred MacMurray. Barbara wasn't a bit like that. Where Hugh's first wife was educated, his second was smart. Big difference. You wonder what a woman like Barbara could have done if she had attended a Vassar or St. Mary's. Hillary Clinton, probably. I remember Barbara used to sound a little Hoosier sometimes, or mispronounce the larger words. She used them correctly, though. Every time. I remember her saying something about somebody being worldly, saying 'eee-rude-ite.' She'd read that word somewhere. But like her husband, she really was a strategist. Nothing much got by her. In her way, Barbara was as brilliant as she was sexually exciting. Like a fly caster, she angled out the line, dangled the bait right where she wanted it. Hugh, curious and hungry, swimming in those rocky shallows, was history."

Six

Shanahan considered himself fortunate to get so much out of an attorney—for free. He wondered how many of Radiquet's old cronies were no longer around. Or, if they were, had retired to a life of golf and chaise lounges in Florida or Arizona.

Outside again. He decided he liked the fresh air. He went for a walk around the Circle. The Circle was the centerpiece of the city. Geographically, it was the actual center of the state. The streets came into the city as spokes on a wheel. Off one spoke was the Capitol. Off another was the old City market. Off another was Circle Center, a conglomeration of shops, cinemas and eateries. The fourth artery led north, passing by still more tributes to Indiana's soldiers, toward the neighborhoods where old wealth and power resided.

On the fourth corner was a beautiful small church attended by many of those who possessed wealth and power. Beside it was the Columbia Club, where Republican men came to eat, drink and determine the future of the city. Women, Shanahan remembered reading, were allowed in the dining rooms these days, but not in 1960. He wondered what Barbara Dart thought about that.

There were those who wanted the brick-lined drive around the Circle for pedestrian traffic only—making it more like a grand European meeting place—an Italian piazza. It was said that the members of the Columbia Club would not permit it. Whether they thought that would attract all sorts of riffraff or were upset only because it would prevent them from parking their Jaguars and BMWs directly out front while they waited for the valet to attend to their car, was not clear.

The Circle was a pleasant place. Low buildings occupied the perimeter of the wide circular drive. Behind those the taller buildings, concrete and marble, sprouted on this particular spot on the prairie. The sky, today, was a pure and innocent blue. The small decorative trees that lined the walk were budding. It was a pretty place and a beautiful day. If Maureen weren't showing a house, she'd be in the garden on a sunny day like this.

Then it hit him. He'd accepted an invitation from Hugh Dart for dinner. He had accepted for himself. The invitation hadn't been extended to Maureen. She was never jealous of his work. In fact, she was far more independent and less demanding than he was.

The real problem was that he was going to a *restaurant* without her. And not just a restaurant but a legendary restaurant. This could be trouble. He could probably go out with another woman more easily than cheat on her with another restaurant.

"Well, I thought you weren't particularly keen on red meat," he could tell her. "Nope. Won't work." She had never been to St. Elmo's—and it was definitely one those places on her ever expanding list. What to do. Could he buy her off with a pint of Häagen-Dazs Swiss Almond Vanilla?

Nope.

Honesty had prevailed. She took it well. A promise of dinner at the California Cafe and a trip to Fletcher's in Atlanta—Atlanta, Indiana—allowed him to leave with a heavy burden lifted from his shoulders.

Shanahan didn't recognize Hugh Dart. There among the eclectic collection of customers waiting to be seated, and the dozen waiters in black tuxes and busboys in double-breasted white jackets, was a splendidly remade Hugh Dart.

"We have a seat," Dart said, grabbing Shanahan and pulling him through the narrow bar.

Two deuces with long white table cloths sat next to each other, a pattern repeated down the length of the bar, leaving a skinny path for patrons, waiters and busboys to collide between the tables and the bar stools.

"What do you think?" Dart asked above the din of clinking glasses and competing conversations.

"About what?"

"About anything, Shanahan. Anything." He raised his glass. "We'll get you a drink. What'll you have?"

"J.W. Dant. Up."

"Good." Dart nodded. He looked different. There was a slight glow to his face. Something had been done to his very short hair to make it look less like a prison cut. He wore a camel-colored blazer that suggested cashmere, though Shanahan never trusted his judgment on such matters. The shirt looked expensive too.

"Prison wages must be pretty good these days," Shanahan said.

Dart managed to snag a waiter. Shanahan looked at the menu. In the dimness, even the large print was a blur. He had remembered his glasses and put them on. They rode down on the end of his nose and he wondered how theatrical that must look.

The steaks first: New York Cut Sirloin, Filet Mignon capped with mushrooms, and Porterhouse. The Porterhouse must have been the three-inch slabs of steak he saw in the glass-enclosed refrigerator everyone passes on the way in. Broiled swordfish "from Florida," and fresh walleye.

"This was my place away from Barbara," Dart said. "Nights with the boys." Shanahan looked around. There still was a scarcity of women in the place—at least in the bar area. There were two more rooms beyond where the women and the less rowdy, non-smoking men dined. "More political deals have been cut here than in the statehouse. After we left here we'd go down to the Brass Rail or go down on the strip and watch the women."

He looked at Shanahan, smiled. "I was young, full of piss and vinegar. Life was rich. In so many ways."

The waiter, old enough to have served Dart on those earlier occasions, set the glass of whiskey on the table.

Shanahan wanted to get right to it. What did Hugh want? Hugh didn't seem to share the sense of urgency. Shanahan could be patient. Maybe he'd even learn something.

They drank awhile without talking. Hugh looked around, taking it all in. Enjoying it. Why not? Shanahan thought. It had to beat the prison mess all to hell. Hugh must be worrying about waking up and finding himself in a cold cell. Thirty-five years of routine isn't easy to forget. On the other hand, Hugh seemed to be doing a pretty good job. He'd already lost that prison pallor and blank look.

Shanahan looked at the menu again. He'd moved away from red meat before he met Maureen. Hard to digest. He thought about the swordfish. Thought maybe the chicken. Pretty stupid coming to a place that specializes in steaks and ordering a chicken breast, particularly at these prices.

He noticed the line on the left of the menu, below a line that spoke of cognacs, armagnacs and port. "Cigar and pipe smoking in the bar only."

The last of the men's clubs, Shanahan thought. The place looked like it should be in Philadelphia, or New York. Who knows? Maybe Boston. Some place East. Not in the Midwest.

There were Hoosier identifying marks, however. There was an old photo of Larry Bird and a very, very young Bobby Knight without the red sweater and pot belly.

The huge clock on the end wall was running about eight hours behind. Seemed appropriate for the place. It was running pretty far behind the rest of the world. So was Hugh. About thirty-five years behind, but catching up fast.

"Used to be darker in here," he said. He nodded toward the dark, porch paneling that ran half way up the bar. Above it were white walls. "Used to be darker in here. So dark, that I might think you're pretty."

Shanahan thought about making some

71

prison comments, thought better of it. But Hugh must have sensed it.

"Nah, Mr. Shanahan. I can't call you that. I can't call you just Shanahan. Don't you have a first name?"

"Dietrich."

Dart made a face. "Can we do better than that?"

"I have a bartender friend. Calls me 'Deets.'"

"Good enough for me. Listen..."

The beginning of the ex-convict's story was interrupted by the waiter. Dart went for the Porterhouse.

"The point of all this..." Shanahan said, then holding his thought so the empty soup bowl could be replaced with a large bowl of extraordinarily plain tossed salad. Iceberg lettuce. Maureen would not have been pleased. "The point of all of this is that you loved her."

"Oooh, OK. Get on with it, right?" Dart was more amused than upset. "Love? Christ. I hated her. It was all passion. All involuntary. What can I say? I couldn't have killed her. To kill her would have been suicidal. She was it for me."

"Sounds like a motive to me."

Dart drained the liquid from his glass. Shook the glass, tried to get more from it.

"You know you can't help who you love. You know them so deeply, love them so deeply, how can you help it?"

"Still sounds like a motive. Maybe she brought out the dark side in you."

"I'm not dark. She is. In places. And you learn to love those dark places. Even if you don't know them."

Shanahan shook his head.

"She was cold, Shanahan. Not Shanahan. Deets. She was cold, Deets. Plots, plans and very, very material dreams."

"She sounds like a very complex person," Shanahan said, trying to take the edge off the sarcasm.

"Yes," Dart said. "In a very mindless way. Now me, I'm simple. Simple people have the grandest ideas."

"They do," Shanahan said, not quite forming a question.

"Yes, what she wanted was a home here— on Meridian. She wanted one in Miami Beach. She wanted a social life, parties, stylish clothes, witty, important people. She wanted the babble of high society."

"And you didn't want that?"

"I didn't care about it. If it made her happy. What I wanted was to serve a president. Chief of Staff, maybe. I wanted to meet the people who shaped history."

"A different kind of babble."

"Yep," he said, sitting back, satisfied with himself and uninterested in the salad.

"All right, let's say you couldn't have killed

her. Impossible. But what's to say someone else didn't kill her?"

"The money's gone, Shanahan. Yeah, well it's easier to call you Shanahan."

"I don't care what you call me. The money's gone. You don't look like you got on what they give you when you leave Michigan City."

"Let me rephrase it then. The big money's gone."

"She's the only one who knew about it, I take it."

"Precisely."

"Maybe she told somebody. They double-crossed her."

"No way. She's too smart, too distrustful."

"You trusted her. And you are smart and distrustful."

"Not her. She's tougher than I am."

"Love makes people do crazy things," Shanahan said, nodding toward Dart. "Look what it made you do."

There was defeat in Dart's smile. "I believe with all my heart that she's alive."

"And the reason you want her found? Love? Again?"

He leaned across the table. "I want my money."

The waiter came to take the empties away. He would be back with brand new drinks.

Smoke rose and hovered a bit over the

tables. The bustle continued. The twosome next to Shanahan and Dart was composed of two men, one of whom was an airline pilot, according to his loud and inebriated monologue. Shanahan hoped he wasn't flying that night or even the next morning.

Dart was just finishing his slab of beef, too busy chewing to be able to talk. And Shanahan didn't know how to do anything other than ask questions. If only Dart could stop chewing long enough to answer the questions. The porterhouse was larger than the pot roast Shanahan's mother used to fix for the family. And that was easily stretched to two meals, maybe three. The roast turned into stew and the stew into hash or vegetable soup. Dart was taking care of his in one sitting.

"This was the only place in town, you know," Dart said, taking a breath and a sip of whiskey. The King Cole is gone. The Shrimp House. "Listen, I'd like you to start right away."

"Why me?"

"Character," Dart said without thinking.

"Character?"

"Absolutely. That's what I was good at in politics and that's how I made it through Michigan City. Judging character. It's simple. You're honest. I need someone honest."

"An honest fool. Easy mark. Why not

Howie Cross?"

"I met him." Dart shook his head. "No. Not what I want."

"Chances are if she's alive she's not around here. You need a big firm. High tech, plenty of branches. This is foolish."

"Listen," Dart started.

"No, wait. Even if I thought I could do it, I wouldn't. I know where you got the money."

Dart laughed. "I understand. It's what an honest person would say. Dirty money. I hate to tell you this." Dart scooted closer to the table. There was a twinkle in his eyes that betrayed his discomfort. He loved what he was doing. "Shanahan, I spent thirty-five years in prison for a crime I didn't commit. Now, wait, wait! I embezzled. True. Couple of million. Number one, that's not a thirty-five-year offense. Two, how much does justice cost? If the police and the judicial system did their job, how much money would they spend to track her down and... and..." he repeated for emphasis, "...to find out who was found in the remains of the fire ... and ... who killed her. Hell, I could sue them for far more than two million."

Again, he sat back, rested his case.

"You were a lawyer?"

"No. Political science. Indiana University. Doesn't take a lawyer to figure this out. Nobody's going to reopen this case. I've been punished. More than punished. I didn't even take parole. I've paid my dues, Shanahan, for a crime I didn't commit. There's a dead woman and a murderer yet to be identified. I want you to help me find them."

"Out of my league," Shanahan said.

"A man can be too honest."

"No. I don't have the resources. And there is a character issue. I don't trust you."

"Here's another approach. I pay you and your friend Howie. Both of you. Now, you work hard to find her. If you can't, then hell I must be guilty or at least I'll know she is dead and some other bum made off with the loot."

"I don't know."

"I remember," Dart said, obviously relishing the recollection, "the day they reported my arrest in the paper, it was Louis B. Mayer's funeral. The movie mogul. Somebody said, 'The reason so many people showed up for his funeral was because they wanted to make sure he was dead.'" He looked at Shanahan. "Maybe I'm wrong. Maybe I should give it up. But I just want to make sure she's dead."

Coffee came. Cognac for Dart. A third whiskey for Shanahan. Both had resisted the New York Cheese Cake, though unlike other restaurants offering a Manhattan version,

77

this one was probably from New York.

"What are your Chicago connections?"

"What?"

"You didn't just decide you wanted to check out tropical Whiting Indiana, did you?"

Dart laughed.

"What if I said I did?"

"Then you'd be lying and there'd be one other reason I couldn't work for you."

"The money was there. Not Whiting. Chicago. I didn't want anyone to know where. Of course only some of the money was there."

"You mean she left some?"

"Yes." He grinned. "To take care of some new clothes and a nice dinner, yes. She didn't look far enough. Actually she looked far enough to get most of it. You've got a lot of questions."

"I've got a few more."

"Shoot."

"The day we were to come up, couple of goons broke into Howie Cross's place, beat him up."

Dart shrugged.

"Nothing to do with you?" Shanahan asked.

"Nothing to do with me. Why would I?"

"Don't know. If you had the money why did you want your daughter to come all the way up to pick you up. Didn't look like to me

78

you were all that happy to see her."

"Ahhhhh, Shanahan." He sighed as if exhausted. "It wasn't my idea in the first place."

"Whose was it?"

"My mother's—" he smiled— "if you can believe that. She thought we had to get together. I didn't care. We have plenty of time, if we want, to mend the relationship. But I really wasn't sure the money would be there. If it wasn't then I had better conserve my pennies. So I took advantage of the offer. Actually, I'm staying at her place. She's never there. She's with your friend Howie." He took a sip, sat back. "If I were a good father, should I be worried?"

"If people keep beating him up, he'd make an ugly son-in-law. The guys who beat up Howie were from Chicago."

"So's Ernie Banks." Not finding a smile on Shanahan's face, Dart forced one himself. "Look, your friend's a private eye. He's got a mouth on him. I'm sure he could make some enemies all on his own. Will you do it?"

"I don't know."

"Think about it, but not too long. I've waited a long time for this and now that I'm out, I'm kind of in a hurry."

"I'll let you know tomorrow."

"If it's the tainted money that bothers you, think about this: Think about my piddley two million dollars and how senators and congressmen are bought and sold every day."

"That doesn't help," Shanahan said.

"Think about this. How much money would you take for thirty-five years of your life and your entire reputation? I can't pick up where I left off. If you think I really did it, why in the hell would I hire you, pay you to find her?"

"Maybe you're looking for something else."

Dart laughed heartily. "I love you Shanahan. You think I'm hiring you to find someone who no longer exists in order for you to find something I've not told you to look for."

Shanahan nodded. "Well..."

Seven

Shanahan knew it the moment his car turned from Washington Street onto his own. The red and blue flashing lights were in front of his own home. He pressed the gas pedal down, then slowed as he approached the group of onlookers.

His heart plummeted, finding its way to his stomach when he saw Lt. Swann come out the front door. Swann was homicide.

Maureen! Now his heart pounded. He met Swann before the cop could slip behind the wheel of the large black Ford Victoria.

"She's fine," Swann said, instantly knowing what was on Shanahan's mind. The lieutenant had sandy hair, worn in a flattop and had a face that looked more Marine recruit than twenty-year police veteran. This was the cop Shanahan trusted. "I heard it come in," Swann said. "Remembered the address. Nobody got hurt here."

Even so, Shanahan moved by him, up the steps and into the front room. A couple of police officers were still there. Maureen seemed calm; but the dog was nervous.

Maureen held him by the collar. A uniformed police officer talked with her.

Shanahan saw his .45 out on the desk.
"What happened?"

Maureen looked up. A grin.

"Two big thugs came in here, took one
look at me and ole Case and flew the coop,"
she said.

"Two guys..."

"Big guys. Eight foot, ten foot, I'm not
sure," she said. "Couple of thousand pounds
each. I took 'em out." She waited, smiling;
but Shanahan was still upset. "Actually they
were in suits. They were a little husky. I
heard the knock, thought you'd forgotten the
key and when I opened the door, they just
kind of barged in. Casey got one of them in
the hand and wouldn't let go. That distract-
ed them long enough for me to get your gun.
Fortunately, they didn't know it wasn't
loaded. They took off."

"Old or young?" Shanahan asked.

"If you let me ask the questions," the
officer said, "I can be on my way a little
sooner. How old were they?"

"In their forties, maybe late thirties.
Husky, like I said, but not that big. Both
were dark. They looked like brothers or
something."

"How tall?"

"Around six foot, both of them."

"No guns?" the officer asked.

82

"None that I could see."

"They say anything?"

"They didn't have a chance. Casey was on the one guy so quick, the only sound I heard was a scream."

"Not bad for an old dog," Shanahan said, watching the dog's bones clunk on the wooden floor. "And so delicate too."

"I can't have this," Shanahan said when they were in bed.

"It's not that serious," Maureen said. She clicked on the television, made the quick transit through the channels. "They won't be back. But it's connected with your date tonight, right?"

"Seems like it. Cross and now you."

"They weren't after me."

"That's the most powerful message they could give me. Threatening you."

"Thanks." She kissed him on the cheek. The TV had landed on *Law & Order*.

There were so many Law & Order shows, Shanahan waited for them to start a new one —*Law & Order, PV*. Parking Violations.

"I had pretty much decided not to take Mr. Dart's offer."

Maureen smiled. "But now you will."

"I have to," Shanahan continued.

"I knew that."

"How did you know that?"

"I know you well enough. You can't be

pushed around," Maureen said.

"I can't?"

"Finessed maybe. When it's done subtly and with a little charm." She kissed him again. "A few drinks, hmmn?" She'd caught the whiff of bourbon.

"A few."

"Well," she said, sweeping the covers off dramatically. "I happen to have a pint of Häagen-Dazs Swiss Almond Vanilla in the freezer. And I'm going to eat every ounce of it."

"That was sudden."

"I've been fighting it all evening. Especially after the uninvited guests arrived. But the police were here and I thought I might be arrested for gluttony."

"You were just afraid you'd have to share."

She was out the door.

He grabbed the remote, searched for a ball game that would play that late. Either one that was going extra innings or a West Coast match-up. Checked out WGN. No Cubs. No White Sox. He caught Letterman. Flicked to Leno. Then back to Letterman.

"I'm going to go jogging tomorrow morning," Maureen said, coming into the bedroom with the pint of ice cream wrapped in a double fold of paper towel. She shoveled a large mound of the white stuff into her mouth. "Mmmmnnn."

"You're going to have to jog to Milwaukee," he said.

The morning ritual was observed. He was out of bed first, leaving Maureen asleep, her auburn hair on the white pillowcase, cheek lovingly against the soft pillow, enjoying her butterfat slumber. Casey was let out the back door to recheck the perimeter fence and re-mark any area that might be fading. Einstein was fed. Salmon, an unappetizing scent this early in the morning. Coffee was ground. Water in the white plastic well. Filter in place. As the coffee brewed and overcame the fishy odor, Shanahan thumbed through the morning *Star*.

He was hungry. He never ate in the morning. But he was hungry. The late dinner last night. The alcohol. They had conspired to shake his routine.

Eggs. Orange juice. Toasted bagels.

"What?" she said groggily, coming into the kitchen.

"Scrambled?" he asked.

"No," she said as if he'd offered her a bag of slimy worms.

He poured her coffee.

"Orange juice?"

"Maybe," she said.

He poured a glass for her.

"Can you go visit your sister?" he asked her.

She laughed. "Why not? There's probably room for me on their little Carnival cruise to the Bahamas. They're probably upset, you know, having to take a honeymoon and just the two of them."

"Well, you could go stay at their place."

"You're always trying to get rid of me."

"Maureen."

"It's not necessary. Lord knows I'm not heroic. But they made their point. They won't be back. And I've got Casey to guard me if they do."

"Maureen, I don't know if—"

"Don't do this to me. This is your job. Let me deal with it. I do want some eggs. Not dry though."

"Don't do this to me," he said in the very same tones she used.

"I'm not trying to be stubborn—"

"No, I mean the eggs. You said you didn't want any. I put everything away."

"Humor me," she said.

He gave her the plate of eggs he'd fixed for himself.

"Shanahan?"

"What?"

"I'll be all right."

Daniel Block was in the phone book. Old North Side address—around 13th, near Central. Shanahan called, explained the situation and Block seemed agreeable.

"Don't know how good my memory is," the *Times* reporter had said, "but maybe a few questions would jog my memory."

"When can I see you?"

"Whenever you want. Go to bed at midnight. Up at six. The rest of the time I'm here, doing a whole helluva lot of nothin'."

The outside of the house had all the gingerbread a Victorian home could handle. Inside, it was plain. Clean, orderly, but plain in the way males often are plain and plain in a way that people accustomed to dealing with just the facts are plain.

Shanahan sat in one upholstered chair in front of a fireplace that showed no signs of recent use. Daniel Block sat in the other. Like Radiquet, Block had thinning hair (but knew it and didn't bother with trying to hide the fact). He was younger than Radiquet. Not much older, if any, than Hugh Dart. Block was pale, thin, wore large, thick-lensed glasses. His face gave away nothing. Shanahan thought he could have been a praying mantis in another life.

"Barbara Dart," Shanahan said.

"Yes." Block nodded. "Colorful. Very colorful. I interviewed Mr. Dart several times in the course of my covering the statehouse and only occasionally ran into the missus. So, I'm not going to be too much help."

"Surely you heard rumors."

"One often hears rumors."

"And..."

"Unsubstantiated. Some of the guys—and it was almost all of the guys in those days covering the statehouse—talked about her and everybody else. The First Ladies garnered most of the attention—all sorts of rumors about alcohol, insanity and infidelity as well as various and sundry supposed scandals about the governors themselves and their cabinets. There were the legislators—a motley crew if there ever was one. Still are, I hear." He smiled.

"Were there any scandals surrounding Hugh Dart?"

"There had been an official investigation of his agency. Money unaccounted for."

"They ever find it?"

"Not to my knowledge."

"Anybody other than Dart investigated?"

"They tried to link it with the Governor. He was having his own problems with the highway scandals. Who knows?"

"You didn't cover the trial?"

"Yes, I did. But there were more questions than answers when the trial was over."

"Who'd Dart hang around with?"

"You know, for someone having Mr. Dart as his client, you're asking an awful lot of questions he could answer."

"People don't remember everything."

"True," Block said. "Dart was one of the young ones. Not so uncommon today, but pretty strange in the sixties. They called Dart 'the kid.' No, they called him the 'Chicago kid,' because he was always up there."

"You said Dart was one of the 'young ones.'"

"There was Pritchardt, another whiz kid, around Dart's age and already had the state hospitals. Couple of the Governor's staffers. And he pal'd around with the State Police and Attorney General. They weren't all that young. Most of those guys are dead."

"Dart made friends that easy?"

"Everybody wants to get close to the Budget Director."

"Could Dart have embezzled through the hospitals?"

"Nothing ever led that way. I always thought there was more bad money in the highway scandal than came out. I mean one little player gets hit for taking a few thousand in bribes. I think millions were involved."

"Do you think Hugh Dart killed his wife?"

"I have no idea. A jury of his peers said he did. I guess that's good enough for me."

"Did you know his first wife?"

"Yes."

"Did you know she went into a mental institution?"

"I heard that."

"What did you know about his wives?"

"Other than that, I don't know. Don't know anything more about either of his wives except that the last one was a looker and she knew it. And of course, that she was murdered."

"Do you know of any other friends Dart had? Or Mrs. Dart for that matter?"

"A lawyer. Don't remember his name..."

"Radiquet?"

"That's it. That's right." Block closed his eyes for a moment. "How could I forget? He was the Clarence Darrow of Indianapolis for awhile. He was the story. He was the story even before Dart. He was bigger than Dart. He got some national coverage. Then, it seemed like after Dart, he kind of just faded or something."

"What about Samuel Dickerson?"

"Sure. Everybody knew Sam. He was on TV for awhile, selling his Studebakers. He still around?"

"He was one of Dart's friends."

"Could be. Probably." Block shook his head and laughed. "Short guy with a bald head and a real hit with the women. If I'm not mistaken he was linked with Barbara Dart. He was a ladies' man. Everybody guessed he had some sort of special secret weapon." Block blushed. "What am I talking about?"

"Talk some more," Shanahan said. "It's important to get all these things off your chest."

"Right," Block said dryly. "The statehouse

90

reporters gossiped a lot, but we didn't let it get too far out of that dreary statehouse basement. We were pretty conservative in those days. Not like Washington. We're still conservative. Some of the stories ... Christ." He shook his head again, remembering. "Even today."

Shanahan wasn't too interested in today's gossip, just that surrounding Hugh Dart and his friends. He wasn't sure the meeting was helpful.

So far, Shanahan had met most of his investigative challenges using the phone book. Now it looked like he'd have to resort to more sophisticated devices. There was no Dr. Augustus Pritchardt and no Samuel Dickerson in the Indianapolis telephone directory.

Eight

More questions for the attorney with the scrapbook. Perhaps he kept track of his old friends.

A phone call, picked up on the third ring. John G. Radiquet was more helpful—though not as much as Shanahan had hoped. He had lost contact with Dr. Pritchardt, had no idea whether the good doctor was even among the living. But at some point, the attorney knew that Pritchardt had moved to Chicago. Perhaps the Chicago phone book, Shanahan thought.

Though Radiquet seemed delighted to hear from Shanahan, Radiquet's voice was slower and his words seemed thicker this afternoon. Some early imbibing. The port, Shanahan remembered, was only an arm's length from Radiquet's desk and a few glasses might seem like the right solution to a long, uneventful afternoon.

Dickerson was an easier task. The attorney had some sort of directory of the city's more important folks. Had a phone number and an address. Dickerson, according to the book that was a decade old, lived on Sunset Lane.

There were a number of Sunset Lanes— and all of them were high rent. The failure of Studebaker must not have taken a serious toll on Mr. Dickerson's future.

"Haven't seen him or talked to him in years," Radiquet said. "We tend to lose track of things and places and people."

On the phone, Dickerson seemed down to earth and friendly—one of those people who acted as if you were already a good friend. He was willing to cooperate and welcomed a visit.

Shanahan was on the short stretch of Sunset that veered off of Spring Mill Road before he realized he'd gotten the wrong one. He pulled into one of the long, straight drives, backed out, headed back down to Kessler. A right, then a left would put him on the right Sunset.

"South of Kessler," Dickerson told him. "I'll be waiting."

This Sunset was the ritziest. There was a sign. Not the usual street sign. This one had gold lettering and said:

Sunset Lane
Blind Road
No Outlet
Residents & Guests Only

All three of the Sunset Lanes had "no outlet." Only this one had other specifications.

The homes on this stretch of Sunset were huge, some set so far off the road that they couldn't be seen. Some set behind great walls. Dickerson's was a little more modest. And, as he said, he was waiting. Outside on the smooth blacktop driveway that lined the long golf-course-type lawn. The driveway disappeared behind a three-story brick home with a gray slate roof. Dickerson wore a pair of tan khaki pants and a salmon-colored knit shirt with the pony on it.

Dickerson was round, tan and bald, except for a neatly cut gray fringe.

It was true. Despite the demise of auto dealership, Dickerson seemed to have fared well. Then again, a lot of time had passed since Studebaker became extinct—plenty enough time to remake a fortune if he had lost it. Some guys, Shanahan thought, went through several fortunes in a lifetime. And the nice thing about the sport of business is that you can compete quite late in life.

Shanahan got out of his somewhat battered '72 Chevy Malibu, thinking he might be lowering the local property values. He introduced himself and told him what he was checking into.

"I've never met a private detective," Dickerson said, extending his hand. "Let's go 'round back and have some coffee and talk about old times. Dart is out, you say?"

"Yes. Served his time."

"'Round back" was a long way. The black-top widened. A four-car garage, also brick with a slate roof, extended from the house. Through a narrow space between them, there was the back yard. There were a few landscaped acres. A pool. A pool house. Some chairs around the pool.

"Get you some coffee?"

"No, I'm fine. I won't take long," Shanahan said. He didn't know why he bothered to use brevity as a lever. Dickerson, like Radiquet, didn't seem to be in any particular hurry.

"Well, shoot!" Dickerson said as they sat under a round table with a large umbrella. "What do you wanna know?"

"About Hugh. And Barbara."

"Well," he said, "where am I gonna start? OK, I was contributing heavily to the Republicans in those days because they were the ones in power. Actually, I don't have a party. Pure capitalist. Anyway, Hugh is the party guy—you know the one you don't see much of, but the one that gets things done. He liked me 'cause I give him money and I liked him because he's gonna make sure the auto business doesn't get screwed by state government."

"So you weren't really best of friends?"

He shook his head. "You know, when you're kids, you got friends and later what you got is allies. Now you might like 'em or you might hate 'em, but they *are* your allies 'cause each of you has mutual interests. Now, if things change, maybe you aren't allies anymore. None of it is personal."

"You and Dart were allies."

"We were allies."

"You haven't talked with him since he was arrested?"

"That's right."

"Barbara Dart?"

"Whew!" Dickerson said. "You know the first time I saw her I said to Hugh, 'Hold her, Newt, she's a rarin'.' Nothing like her ever in this world."

"She kind of got around, didn't she?" Shanahan asked.

"No doubt."

"With you?"

"A gentleman doesn't tell," Dickerson said, smiling.

"Word is out that you got along fine with the ladies."

"I confess. I did then. Times change. Married to the same woman all my life. Kids. Grand kids. The little ones, they are my life now. Don't get me wrong, I didn't find religion all of a sudden and I probably get a mild case of whiplash now and then when a pretty girl goes by, but I'm toeing the line."

"Your thoughts on what happened?"

"Between Hugh and Barbara?" He rubbed his palm back over his forehead like he was brushing the hair out of his eyes. But there was none to brush. "Hmmn, don't know for sure. But the jury said he killed her. The boy was a pragmatist. Could have done it. On the other hand, if I were a bettin' man, I woulda bet he woulda got by with it if he did it."

"What?"

"If he'd planned to do such a thing, he'd've done it without getting caught."

"Anybody want to see him hang?"

"You make enemies in his business."

"Anybody I should know about?"

He shrugged. "Too many years have passed. If there was somebody, he's probably dead. So he's hired you to find the real killer—like *The Fugitive*? The one-armed man?"

"No, he's hired me to find his wife, Barbara."

"No!" he said excitedly. He leaned over the table. "The boy wonder is bonkers. Then again, why else would you be looking into it?"

"Could she have set him up?"

Dickerson laughed heartily. "Oh, she was smart, don't let me imply she wasn't. But that'd have been a good one." He shook his head. "Wow!"

"She never told you anything in those

intimate moments, Mr. Dickerson?"

"The sweet nothings she whispered in my ear had nothing to do with murder, Mr. Shanahan."

"So you don't see any of the old gang anymore—Radiquet or Dr. Pritchardt?"

"Nope. My life's all different now. I spend half my time in Florida. Come back up here in the spring. I'd stay down there all the time. Hell, it's just as hot up here in the summer as it is down there. But the wife wants to be with the grand kids. They're up here. So we come back."

"Real quiet life now."

"Yeah, I'm in the protection mode now. Some golf up the street there. Family. Lots of family."

"What does 'protection mode' mean?"

"That means I'm not as interested in makin' money as I am in protecting it. Passing it along to the right people without giving most of it away to Uncle Sam. Lots of legal stuff now. Trusts. Living trusts. That kind of stuff. I'm not involved in anything risky. And I don't plan on being. I know just where I am in life, Mr. Shanahan. And it isn't staying too long at the roulette table."

"Dr. Pritchardt. You have any idea where I might find him?"

"Haven't seen old Augie in years. Then again, I haven't seen him in the obits either. Don't know."

"You know who would know?"

Dickerson thought a moment. "Maybe Radiquet. Check the university. It's been awhile though. I haven't heard anything from him or about him in twenty years anyway. Frankly, I haven't thought much about him. He was closer to Dart than me. He had a superior attitude. Thought I was a little too common. That's one thing you can say about Hugh. He didn't look at how much education you had or what kind of family background you came from, just how much money you had."

"True American," Shanahan said.

Dickerson laughed, continued. "I mean, look at what happened. He dumped his first wife and her money and her pedigree for Barbara, who was wearing icing and little else when they first met. And Barb didn't exactly speak the King's English—at least at first. And sure as hell, she didn't come from money. But that's what she wanted. Money and legitimacy."

"You've done all right too. I don't mean to be too nosy," Shanahan said, "but you seem to have done all right for a car dealer whose product went down the toilet."

"Good observation. I didn't lose anything. I wasn't in debt. My property was worth a fortune. I just moved on. Damned shame too. Studebaker was a helluva car in its time."

"I agree."

"You want to see a little memento of my days as a car salesman?" Dickerson seemed to relish calling himself a "car salesman."

Shanahan followed Dickerson through the side door of the huge garage. There was a silver Volvo station wagon. A silver Mercedes sedan. A fairly late model Cadillac and, in the far stall, was a black Studebaker.

"Silver Hawk," Dickerson said. "1956. Ten years later, Studebaker shriveled up and died in Canada."

Shanahan admired the immaculate two-door, one that outfinned the "forward look" of the Chrysler that year. The Silver Hawk was far more elegant too. Its sweeping, aerodynamic design looked as fresh today as it did then. Shanahan finally found something to envy.

"They had an electric Studebaker," Dickerson said. "Did you know that? Turn of the century. Studebaker was the largest car company in the world. Right up the street in South Bend, Indiana. Studebaker owned Pierce Arrow." Dickerson ran his hand along the long shiny fin. "Used to have a small collection, but I whittled it down to this one. Took up too much of my time. This is it. My baby. This and my grand kids. That keeps me going. Want to take a spin?"

"No," Shanahan said. "It'd make me want it too much. You wouldn't consider a trade would you?"

Dickerson smiled.

"You have any holdings in Chicago?" Shanahan asked.

"Probably. I don't really know."

"I thought you kept close track of all of this."

"Nothing direct, Mr. Shanahan. I have all sorts of investments and I'm sure I've got some ties to Chicago. But then I've probably got ties to Karachi, Cucamonga and Timbuktu and I don't even know it."

"Let me know if you think of anything. I'm in the book."

"So, Mr. Shanahan," Dickerson said, walking him back to his car, the asphalt beginning to smell from a surprisingly strong sun, "you buying this 'Barbara is still alive' thing? You just working for Dart because it's a job or do you believe him?"

"Damned if I know."

"He has a way about him," Dickerson said. "Watch out."

Time for lunch, Shanahan thought, walking down the blacktop. So thick. In July, you'd probably sink through it—a black, oily quicksand. Did he want something good to eat? Or did he want to go somewhere where he could relax? He chose comfort over taste.

Harry had a few customers. One was in a booth. He had been conned into the stew and was using his spoon to probe the contents in search of something that might be edible. There was a middle-aged couple at the far booth who looked a little down and out. Whatever they were talking about was apparently in the life and death league, judging by the intensity of their conversation.

Murph occupied a stool at the far end of the bar, half hidden in the darkness of the nook between the bar and the entryway. As far as Shanahan knew, Murph had been sitting there from 11 A.M. to roughly 4 P.M. every day but Sunday for ten years, beginning shortly after he retired. It was Delaney's Bar then. But it didn't matter, nothing changed except the stew. Certainly not Murph's seat. Not his bottles of Budweiser which he peeled as he pondered God knew what.

"Don't you ever feel guilty?" Shanahan asked Harry.

"Which specific cardinal sin that I have committed are you referring to?"

"Murph. Letting him drink himself into oblivion."

"Since when did you become so highfalutin' moral?"

"I'm not judging. Just asking."

"You take the cake, sometimes," Harry said, shaking his head.

"Harry, listen. I'm just trying to figure

102

something out, that's all."

"You know how many bars like this one are out here? Just in this neighborhood?"

"I don't know."

"Thirty, fifty. Now, I throw Murph outta here and he's gonna walk a block or two farther up or down and settle in and drink himself into oblivion. Every damn one of them's got at least one Murph. Am I doing him harm? Yeah." Harry shrugged. "But, Murph don't drive. He don't get mean. And it's unlikely I'm gonna get him to drink Shirley Temples and go to Sunday school. You want to do that, go ahead. He's sittin' right over there, ripe for your missionary ways."

"OK. Never mind."

Harry left to wipe off the bar. Nothing to wipe, but it got him away from his anger. He came back after every surface had been gone over at least twice.

"So you're feeling guilty about something?" Harry set down a bottle of Miller and a shot of J.W. Dant.

"Yep," Shanahan said.

"Mr. Dart, I suppose."

"Yep."

"Going to pay you in dirty money?"

"Yep."

"Well, you're in a fix, aren't you?"

"Yep."

"I don't know what to say."

"Damn," Shanahan said. "That's never happened before. This just may be a sign the world's coming to an end."

"Why are you even considering it? I mean you've always been kind of a prude."

"Dart's argument is that if he didn't kill his wife, thirty-five years in jail ought to be worth something. So he's entitled to the money."

"That'd be enough for me."

"But maybe he killed his wife."

"Don't make no sense. He's asking you to find her."

"Yeah."

"Are you gonna do it?"

"I'm already doing it. I just haven't told Dart yet."

"Hey, Harry!" yelled Murph. "Can you get another one down here pretty soon?"

"Be right with you."

"What does he do on Sunday when you're closed?" Shanahan asked.

"Hey, Murph, what do you do on Sunday?"

"I've gotta a Bible reading class down on Euclid."

Nine

"Hugh Dart wants you to call him," Maureen said when Shanahan came into the kitchen, right before she placed a small kiss on his cheek. She handed him a slip of paper.

Shanahan went to his desk in the living room, dialed. A woman answered. Didn't sound like Melanie. An older woman.

"Is Hugh there?"

"Just a moment."

Maureen filled in the silence of the phone.

"Dinner with me tonight. Tell Dart he can find his own date," Maureen said, whisking by on her way out the screen door to the back yard, Casey following.

Einstein landed on the desk, pushing a small stack of papers off the edge.

"This is Hugh."

"Shanahan."

"In or out, Shanahan?"

"In."

"Good," Dart said, sounding genuinely pleased. "What's next?"

"Why don't we get together for an hour or so? Maybe I can get an honest recounting of

105

your past?"

"Haven't I been honest?"

"You had a wife before Barbara."

He laughed. "I had a girlfriend in the fifth grade. Her name was Jean Marie. She asked me to kiss her. And when I did, she slapped me. That was, unfortunately, one of the many lessons I didn't take to heart. Anyway, I can tell you a lot; but I don't have time for a detailed discussion of my stamp collection."

"Where is she now?"

"Dunno."

"Where is Dr. Pritchard?"

"Dunno. Listen, why don't you come over here. You can meet my mother. You can ask her what my first words were and what I thought about strained carrots."

"Deal."

Shanahan told Maureen about the guys—Radiquet, Dickerson and the long lost Dr. Augustus Pritchardt. He told her he had one more stop to make—to meet Hugh's mother. Maureen laughed. "He's staying with his mother?"

"He hasn't seen her in a while," Shanahan said. "He doesn't have many friends."

Maureen was satisfied with a promise to have dinner at Sakura's.

"You want me to find Dr. Pritchardt?"

"Sure," Shanahan said. "And while you're

at it," he said sarcastically, "get his address and his phone number, would you?"

"His father and I knew that Hugh wouldn't become a minister," she said. "We knew that early on. Murder though? No." She smiled, looked at her son who nursed a glass of clear liquid Shanahan guessed was gin. "Larceny, perhaps."

Mrs. Dart was an attractive lady. Disarmingly frank with a touch of humor. She sat in a wheelchair, the battery beneath looking like it could take a trip to Memphis and back without recharging.

"I don't think he came here for a character reference, Mom," Dart said. "Not that you'd be very helpful."

"Actually I came to ask your son a few more questions."

"You're working on his case?" she asked.

"Depends on his answers."

The house wasn't far from Shanahan's. Eastside. A block off Pleasant Run Parkway. A small, but sturdy brick home on a small hill. Inside, the small rooms were done in light rose wallpaper and muted tones of darker rose and green tones of upholstered ornate furniture.

"I can't hire him until I prove myself innocent, something I had a little trouble with thirty or so years ago." Dart took a sip. "Shoot."

"I haven't had a chance to look at the trial or your file, Hugh. But you didn't have an alibi for the night your wife was killed?"

"She wasn't killed."

"Doesn't matter at the moment."

"I told the court I was out driving."

"And?"

"I was." He looked at his mother. He took another hit from the glass, this time a little deeper.

"Out, roaming around? Just driving?" Shanahan didn't believe his answer.

"We had a little spat, Barbara and I. I went out to cool off."

"In January?"

"Yes."

"It was frigid and icy outside. And you went out for a drive? Just for a drive?"

"Yes."

"Why don't I believe you?"

"Because he's not telling the truth," Mrs. Dart said. "It's written all over his little face."

"It's in the court records, Mother," Hugh said sternly.

"Mr. O.J. Simpson was playing golf. That was in the court records too. Playing golf at night while he was also napping, showering and packing to catch a plane."

"Why don't you drive into your bedroom and darn some socks, Mother?" he said, smiling.

"I'm puzzled why you want to even hire me, Mr. Dart. But there's no way I can work for you unless I get the truth..."

"...the whole truth and nothing but the..." Mrs. Dart said.

"My trial. What I said or didn't say on the stand has nothing to do with what I've hired you to do, which is to find Barbara."

"Even if she's alive there may be no way to find her, Mr. Dart. Maybe, just maybe there's one little, tiny, clue. And that clue may be hidden in something you consider to be irrelevant."

"OK. I was visiting a prostitute in Terre Haute. I told Radiquet that. He said that would only make matters worse."

"A genuine alibi," Shanahan said. "That would make matters worse?"

"Radiquet said no one would believe her and that admitting that kind of liaison would go against my character. Further, when I got off, which he assured me I would, I would have ruined any possibility of getting back my reputation."

"What was her name?" Shanahan asked.

"I don't remember."

Shanahan shrugged.

"It's been a long time."

"How did you find her?" Shanahan asked.

"It wasn't the first time I had seen her. Shirley. Shirley was her name. Last name? Don't ask. Shirley probably wasn't her real name anyway."

"Do you have an address?"

"Yeah, right."

"How old was she?"

"I don't know."

"Older or younger than you were?"

"Younger." Hugh smiled. "She was pretty nice. Wasn't a real blonde, you know?" He looked at his mom, then at Shanahan.

"Like I said," Mrs. Dart responded with a grin, "we knew he wasn't going to be a saint. I could tell that before he learned to walk. But he wouldn't have hurt anyone, let alone kill anyone. You can tell that too. Very early on."

"Mrs. Dart, who might know something about Barbara? Nobody seems to know much about her except for your son. Who would she talk to? Her mother?"

"I'm not sure Barbara ever knew her mother. She was in a series of foster homes somewhere in New Jersey, I think. She never talked about them. She didn't talk to me. I don't think she had many friends. Really. Kind of sad."

"She had some friend in Omaha or Tulsa or something," Hugh Dart said. "She called a couple of times. I think they corresponded."

"Yes. Karen something," Mrs. Dart said. "We can find out. Her letters are upstairs in the attic."

"What?" Shanahan asked.

"After the fire, there were some personal possessions of Barbara's," Mrs. Dart said. "No one knew what to do with them. We brought them here."

"The fire didn't destroy them?"

"The fire destroyed the first and second floors, but not a lot of the basement. Water damage, but these were in a metal container."

"And you still have them?" Hugh asked his mother.

"I never felt quite right about throwing them away. What if a relative showed up? There was nothing left of her as it was."

"Have you read them?"

"Certainly not. They weren't addressed to me."

"Barbara will be grateful you were so thoughtful," Hugh said.

"Why don't you go get me a drink, Hugh? One of those things."

"A martini?"

"Yes. A martini. I've always wanted to try one."

"Maybe I should just go darn some socks," he said.

"That would be nice, Hugh. Take your time."

"May I look through those letters?" Shanahan asked.

"Of course you may," she said, but her

tone was now all business. "Let me tell you two things. Quickly. One. Hugh was madly in love with her. Madly. His heart and soul. He didn't kill her. But, number two. She's dead. Probably one of her lovers."

"What lovers?"

"Didn't know them. But you could tell. She was a sensuous, needy woman, Mr. Shanahan. She would not have gone without. And he was sleeping on the sofa and finally made other arrangements as you are now quite aware."

"So? What would you like me to do?"

"You seem like a nice man. Be a friend for a while. I'm afraid what will happen if he doesn't face the fact that she's dead. I'm afraid what will happen if he does."

There was something about seeing a man with his mother that was demystifying. Whatever edge Hugh Dart seemed to have was slipping away, which also had the effect of making it seem less likely the man would kill his wife—at least intentionally.

Ten

Maureen sat there with her plate of sushi, deftly plucking morsels with her chopsticks.

Shanahan had been more daring than usual. He was drinking the Asahi—not his usual Miller's—with his chicken teriyaki.

"How'd it go?"

"Fairly well. I have some letters to go through from a friend of Barbara's. I've got further testimony that Hugh Dart is a rascal but not a Rasputin. But I've also got word from his mother that the lovely wife was murdered, though by somebody else—one of her lovers."

Maureen raised her eyebrows. "You believe her?"

"I don't know. She's believable. Meanwhile, Hugh's alibi is that he was seeing a woman of the evening in faraway Terre Haute at the time."

"Oh?"

"Information not used at the trial. Her name is Shirley. After thirty years who knows where she is?"

"This little ditty is littered with missing

people. What would you give me for the whereabouts of Dr. Augustus Pritchardt?" She pinned a cucumber roll between the little wooden sticks and set it down on the edge of Shanahan's plate of teriyaki.

"The moon."

"Full moon," she said. "Nothing short of a full moon."

"Sure. Of course. I'll throw in the stars. Oh hell, the solar system. But if you think you're getting the universe, young woman, you have another think coming."

Maureen reached in her purse and pulled out a slip of paper. "Fifteen-fifty North State Parkway, Chicago. The apartment number is on the slip."

"How?"

"Physicians usually belong to organizations. Organizations have publications. Publications have mailing lists. Sometimes you just have to call them to make sure they have your correct address. 'Mrs. Sanderson for Dr. Augustus Pritchardt. What address do you show because we have not received the last two issues?'"

"Chicago," Shanahan said. He thought perhaps things were coming together.

"What are you thinking?"

"I'm not sure. But all roads lead to Chicago."

"No phone number. I couldn't figure out how to do that."

"You did really well."

"I made reservations for two at a small hotel and got us very cheap flights for tomorrow, leaving around noon. I thought I would shop, eat at Bice and you could traipse around and ask strangers strange questions."

"That might be fun."

"Except I can't go."

"Why?"

"House. A closing. They changed the time. I canceled my flight."

"I don't want you here alone," he said.

"Now you're being sexist. You let Howie stay alone."

"I'm not in love with Howie."

"How sweet," she said.

"Though if he had a little more hair and dropped a few pounds..."

"Shut up. Better think about how you're going to pay me what you owe me." She took a swig of his beer.

In the darkness of his bedroom, Howie and Melanie kissed. He felt a dull pain. "Bastards," he uttered in his brain, more anger than passion despite her caresses.

"You OK?" she asked.

"A little residual irritation," he said to her. He couldn't see her, but felt her breath.

"I'm sorry." She kissed him lightly. "Better?"

115

"Better," he said, but he didn't mean it.

His head fell back on the pillow. She remained above him, more presence than form.

"I know you don't want to go into this," he said with a sigh.

"If we're about to embark on a sentimental journey to my childhood, you're absolutely right."

"Well, let's not make it sentimental."

"Let's just not make it."

"You are so soft and warm. Then *wham*, you are chilly."

She laughed. "That's me."

"And evasive."

"That's me."

"And secretive."

"I am all of those things. That's what I am. It's part of me. Part of what you'll have to weigh up when you think about whether or not you want to see me again."

"True. But this presents a problem. The essence of me is curiosity. I like to know what's in the cave or behind the locked door or in the chest at the bottom of the sea."

"We're made for each other, then?"

"All right, let me change the subject. How are the two of you getting along?"

"The two of what?"

"Your dad and you?"

"I thought we were changing the subject."

"This isn't childhood stuff. This is yesterday, maybe the day before. Not exactly a journey back in time."

"We don't see each other. I think we both like it that way."

"You don't want to get to know him?"

"I know enough."

"Here," Shanahan said, handing his bed partner a letter from the small stack.

"Shouldn't this be confidential?" Maureen asked.

"Probably. She's supposed to be dead. This is material for my investigation. I'm considering you a consultant. Maybe, as a woman, you'll be better at reading between the lines."

"Maybe," she said.

The Cubs game, a night game in San Francisco was in the top of the eighth. It was only a mild distraction. The Cubs were behind eleven to one.

Shanahan had gotten little from the first letter he'd pulled from the slender stack, held together by an inexpensive gold ribbon. Each envelope had been opened neatly, slit along the top, and each letter appeared to have been refolded neatly and placed back inside. The first installment of half a dozen yielded little.

A change of address from Karen Stillman. From Jersey City to Omaha. The date coincided with the first year or so of Barbara's

117

marriage to Hugh. "Tell me more, 'Mrs. Dart,'" was the only reference beyond Karen's full and most recent biography.

The second letter was more revealing:

Dear Barbara—

So you've done it. I am surprised. I would never have thought you would settle in such a small town, let alone marry. He sounds exciting, though. And knowing you, you will harness his ambition so that it might carry you to your dreams. I can't help but remember your admonitions about men (not that I needed them) while I read such carryings on about how wonderful this Hugh fellow is.

I am just jealous of course. You are in Indianapolis and I am in Omaha. So far from the beaches and nightclubs of Miami. I wonder who will get there first. No, I don't. You will, of course.

As for me, I am working in a factory. Don't scoff. The money is excellent and I don't have to sell body and soul to make the rent. But I am through with Harrison. On my own. He turned out to be another boob.

Keep in touch.
Karen

The rest of the letters were similar. Envying Barbara. Being burnt by men. Boredom with the town and with the job. Remembering with a mix of horror and humor their time together as "sisters" in one of the families they had in common. The last letter was slightly different:

Dear Barbara—

I have to tell you something very important. I don't know who else to tell. There is no one else in my life except you and the person I'm going to tell you about.

Her name is Linda. And we love each other. I suppose I knew that something like this would happen. I have known this side of myself for a long time. Even while I knew you. In fact ... You can probably fill in the rest of the sentence.

Whether you know it or not, you have kept me afloat during my roughest times. When it was the most bleak, I could think of the two of us in Miami Beach under the sun and near the shining waters, laughing together. Or a night, under a starry sky with a Latin beat behind us and the whole world ahead of us. It was my fantasy. And it sustained me. You are so wonderful and so beautiful.

So I wanted to tell you. Still, not having spoken to you directly for so long, I have been scared to call you and talk to you in person. Linda and I are moving to New Mexico. She wants to paint and I just want to be with her.

I will write and give you our address as soon as we are settled.

I am sorry that your life isn't moving in the direction you want. But have patience. I know that it will. You have always found a way to get what you want. I'm not sure you liked men any more than I did; but you did know how to handle them. I so admired that.

I am so sure you will have all the diamonds you can handle and a mansion on Miami Beach.

Best wishes to you, my other love,
Karen

"What do you think?" Shanahan asked as Maureen put down the last letter.

"I don't know. Opens up some possibilities."

"Thirty years of possibilities."

"'My other love,' she says."

"Yes. New Mexico. Miami. The rest of the world. If she were still alive she could be in Paris or Morocco."

"Or Omaha."

Eleven

The flight from Indianapolis to Chicago's Midway was short and choppy. The train ride from the airport to the Loop seemed longer and smoother. And certainly more scenic. The train passed a series of dilapidated warehouses, graffiti-faced walls, railroad-flat residences, unattractive but functional playgrounds, auto graveyards, boarded-up high-rises. Tough city, Chicago.

He remembered coming into Chicago when he was a kid. Not from this direction, though. From the north, to see the Cubs games. He lived closer to Milwaukee, but Milwaukee didn't have the Brewers then. They didn't even have the Braves. Even so, he remembered the Chicago people. Tough, hamfisted. Muscles they got from work not from working out in air-conditioned gyms. The city outside his train window seemed to say that.

The Orange line cut into the city itself, cut into the downtown. The high-rises were gray needles pricking an opaque sky. There weren't buildings like these anywhere else in the Midwest. Not like the library building, huge and forbidding, gargoyles roosting on the corners. Not like the "Metropolitan Correctional Facility," a huge lump of a building that looked more like an above-ground tomb than a prison.

The train, well above street level, snaked by office buildings, giving the riders a glimpse into the windows, though most looks were the same—fluorescent lights, computers and padded cubicles.

Sparks flew from steel wheels on the metal tracks as the train threaded its way above the traffic through the skyscrapers until it came to his stop. Shanahan walked down into the drizzle to catch a taxi.

The view changed. Out on Lakeshore there was the other Chicago, one more dominated by wealth and power, a Chicago possessing an awesome, if not quite elegant presence.

The taxi took him from the appointed stop in the Loop to his hotel. He was there only long enough to check in and drop his luggage in his small room. He should have kept the cab. The desk clerk said he could call for one; but that it might take a while because of the rain. Shanahan would have a better chance, the clerk said, by going out on Broadway and flagging one down himself.

Shanahan, after waiting in Chicago's version of April showers, had the Checker drop him a few blocks away from the address, on the corner of State and Goethe, between the Ambassadors, the hotels that were east and west of State Street. It was an old habit, one from his Army intelligence days. Find out if you are being followed before you arrive at your destination.

Who would have followed him? Whoever did the job on Howie's face. Whoever invaded his house. It was clear someone was interested in something. And Shanahan didn't want to give whatever in the hell it was away.

He walked down State Street. Grand apartment houses with doormen and grand, sturdy homes up handsome steps to grand entrances. Gardeners were putting in flowers. Bright colors struggled in the damp gloom of the day.

"My gloom," Shanahan said. He wanted very much to be home with Maureen. Or perhaps better, to have Maureen along with him. She was the one that made him feel again. It was her fault that he now felt the sadness of the day, the sadness of being alone. Before her he had merely accepted the sense of being alone as the state of his being.

Here it was. A tall building faced in stone. Probably built around the time Shanahan was born, but in better condition. From the outside he could see that each corner apartment had a five-window bay and French doors leading out to a small balcony guarded by a wrought-iron grille.

The door was around the corner on North Street. Fortunately for Shanahan, the front door was open—no doubt as an accommodation to a young Hispanic preparing a dark, humus-rich plot of earth for some sort of planting.

Shanahan nodded toward the youth. Got nothing in return. He entered the dark, cool stone lobby.

There was no answer at the door. Shanahan looked at his watch. It was 4:30. If Pritchardt was still a professor, then he might be home soon. If he were a practicing doctor it would be difficult to predict. There was no guarantee he was even in town. Shanahan thought of coming back later. If he left, though, he might not be able to get back into the building. And if he merely confronted Dr. Pritchardt's voice from the downstairs telephone, rejection was more likely. He decided to wait.

He sat on the window ledge, now feeling both warm and damp, readying a reason for loitering if someone should ask. It was quiet. The first person he saw was a black woman carrying a plastic bag that strained where she gripped it. She noticed Shanahan but did not acknowledge him as she passed. She looked his way at least twice while she waited for the elevator.

An elderly woman got off the elevator some minutes later. She too took notice of the man at the end of the hall; but didn't seem fearful. Seventy-year-old men aren't likely muggers, Shanahan thought. However, he did hear three locks click into place after her door shut.

It was nearly seven before another person arrived on the floor. Shanahan waited. Male, about sixty-five or so. Could easily be the doctor; though Shanahan pictured Augustus to be a big man, robust, dominating. The man in the 35-year-old newspaper clipping appeared to be heading in that direction. This man, clutching a heavily weighted, heavily worn satchel-type briefcase, was tall enough, but exceedingly slender. Drawn. He had the key to Pritchardt's apartment, though. Therefore...

Shanahan moved up the hall, catching Pritchardt before he got the door open.

"Yes?" Pritchardt asked as Shanahan approached. The door was open. Key chain still dangled from the lock.

"My name is Dietrich Shanahan. I'm a private investigator."

Pritchardt's eyes widened. Shanahan could not tell whether it was surprise, fear or madness. The look on the doctor's face was disturbing.

"Yes," Pritchardt said with an implied, "go on."

"I'm investigating the death of Barbara Dart." The doctor's eyes widened again. "I wonder if we could talk," Shanahan continued.

"I see no point to that," he said, eyes normal again, uninterested. "She's quite dead. Has been so for a couple of decades. So I'm afraid you are a bit tardy in your investigation."

"I understand your position. I read the papers. Hugh Dart, however, is convinced that the murder victim was not his wife."

When Pritchardt's eyes again widened, the pattern was clearer. New or unsuspected information caused a moment's alarm.

"Well, I assure you it was." Pritchardt attempted to squeeze through a narrow opening into his apartment, making it clear there wasn't room for two in the process.

"How can you do that?" Shanahan asked. "Be so sure."

"Who else could it be?"

"That's what I'm trying to find out."

"This is all in the past," Pritchardt said, closing the door. "I see no need to dredge all this up."

The door was shut.

Shanahan had gotten nothing.

The door opened. Shanahan could see only a sliver of the doctor's face.

"Hugh is out?"

"Yes."

"This is Hugh's idea?"

"Yes."

"Where is he?"

"I'd be glad to exchange information if we could possibly sit down. I've been walking quite awhile, waiting even longer—and I'm afraid I need to use a bathroom."

Pritchardt's home was dark, heavy and brooding. On the walls were paintings, all representing a period when artists perceived human flesh to be pale and tinted blue, and the times as tortuous and full of sorrow.

Shanahan wondered how someone could live in these morbid surroundings. He wondered if part of Pritchardt's teaching had been the dissection of bodies. Didn't medical school include cadavers and body parts? Did his students practice surgery? Strange, Shanahan thought, but someone had to do the jobs others found macabre—working in a slaughterhouse, a mortician, a professor who carved classroom corpses. All in a day's work. Everyone had a job to do.

Then again, someone could easily question Shanahan's vocation. A lot of what he saw was squalid and sleazy. His jobs were not without frequent exposure to human suffering. Worse, he had often caused it. He'd been accused more than once of meddling, sticking his nose into other people's business. Wasn't he little more than a licensed peeping Tom?

Shanahan looked at the art again. He was no judge of art, but if he had to guess, he'd bet these were originals. And expensive ones at that. In fact, the hall that led from the bathroom and the living room was full of bronze statues and expensive-looking bric-a-brac. The furniture was rich and thickly upholstered. Everything was heavy and dark. The room itself seemed both serious and sad.

Pritchardt sat on the edge of one of the large chairs, perched, it seemed, almost like a bird ready to take flight at a strange sound or shadow.

"How did you find me?" he asked.

"Were you hiding?" Shanahan asked. He wasn't offered a chair, but he took it.

"No, of course not. It's just that I've not heard from anyone in such a long time, I was sure I was out of all of my past realms."

"Meaning what?"

"The past. The people. Hugh Dart to be specific. He's out of prison?"

"Completed his sentence. A free man. And interested in what he refers to as Barbara's disappearance. As I said before, he believes his wife is still alive."

"Well, there was an autopsy."

"Yes. Apparently that didn't change his mind."

"He's not a doctor, is he? You aren't either,

are you?" Pritchardt asked, but didn't wait for a response. "So that the matters of death and identity shouldn't be left to you, should they? Or him? Don't you think?"

"I don't know what to think," Shanahan said.

"And I would still like to know how you found me," the doctor demanded, suddenly busying himself with cleaning his eyeglasses.

"You're not an investigator are you, Mr. Pritchardt? Let's just leave that to the professional, wouldn't you say?"

Pritchardt seemed like a lonely, frightened man at first and Shanahan tried not to dislike him. But it was becoming more difficult.

"Does Hugh know where I live?"

"Why do you care? Is there a reason for you to be frightened of him?"

"If you don't answer my questions, I shall not answer yours." He stood up.

"At the moment, no," Shanahan said calmly. "He doesn't know where you live. Actually I'm not working for him. Officially that is. I'm trying to figure out whether his claims have merit."

"They do not."

"My turn. What makes you think Hugh killed his wife?"

"It's not my opinion. After the presentation of evidence, a jury of his peers apparently came to that conclusion."

"Relax a little, OK. I'm just trying to get a

feel for all of this." Pritchardt sat down again, still taking his precarious perch. "So you and Hugh and Dickerson and Radiquet all hung out together?"

"Hugh was the glue that held us together," Pritchardt said. "Though I found Mr. Radiquet interesting enough in conversation I'm not sure we would have become fast friends on our own. And most certainly Mr. Dickerson and I wouldn't have had much to do with each other at all. We were odd pieces in Hugh's eclectic collection of people and things. Until Barbara."

"And she broke up the little gang of yours?"

"She was something," he said, seeming to drift into a memory. "She took the attention away from Hugh. She was as magnetic, as electric. She stole our concentration, our will."

"Pretty talented lady."

He shrugged in an attempt to dismiss the importance he had given it. "They were quite a couple. When that all happened. Her death. His conviction. It was like all the air had gone out of our lives." He corrected himself. "Mine anyway."

"Why would he kill her?"

"If Hugh believes she was killed by someone else, whom does he suspect?"

"He believes she's not dead."

"Oh, of course, you've said that. So, I take

it we are to ignore the fact there was a corpse."

"You seem to have done well for yourself," Shanahan said after a moment of quiet awkwardness.

"Not that well."

"A professor, right?"

"Yes. I'm prudent, Mr. Shanahan. And it is not your business anyway."

"She is alive, isn't she?"

"Don't be ridiculous."

"Dart seems convincing."

"Hugh has always been convincing. He can have you believe whatever he wants you to believe. Apparently prison hasn't robbed him of his gift." Pritchardt stood. "I'm going to ask you to leave now. While you are in Chicago you should visit the Art Institute. It's quite nice. There's a new exhibition," he said, "if you are one of those who enjoy contemporary art."

Twelve

The Kung Pao chicken wasn't very good. He had stood between a Japanese and Chinese restaurant on one of Chicago's busier streets, trying to decide and most likely made the wrong decision. Maureen had always told him never to eat at any restaurant that felt obliged to show a photograph of the food. He had gone against her rule and lost.

Then torrents of rain caught him as he left the restaurant and made his way back to the hotel. He took off his damp clothes, took a warm shower and climbed into bed. He flipped through the channels—news, religion, movies. He spent a few moments trying to catch glimpses of clarity in a scrambled adult channel. He really didn't want to watch an X-rated movie. But attempting to see what was intentionally, electronically obfuscated was a challenge he found difficult to resist. He propped up his pillow and sat back, muting the moans of pleasure, so no passerby in the hall would think his mission was prurient.

There were moments when an object would be clear, recognizable. There were moments when something he had identified as one thing was actually another when the frame straightened for a moment. It was obvious that a few suggestions, combined with his imagination, could manifest just about anything. Something he saw as an extremely sexually graphic sexual act turned out to be a man caressing a woman's cheek.

At least half of what people see are what they want to see, he thought. He shut off the set, rearranged the pillows and was adrift before he turned off the light, all the while convinced that after thirty years it was all too easy to build another story using the same information. Shanahan believed that Hugh was slightly crazy now, that Barbara Dart was at this moment being absorbed by earth.

Shanahan was only occasionally conscious of his dreams. But when he woke in the middle of the night the dream, or at least part of it, was vivid. So was the congestion in his chest and head, which had no doubt come from the damp and chilly evening before.

A zombie-like Pritchardt was performing surgery on a corpse and the body was Maureen's.

He reached for the phone. He realized he could not see the numbers on the buttons, let alone read the instructions for long-distance calls. He crawled out of bed, bones aching, looking for his jacket so that he could get his reading glasses.

He was perspiring. He was weak. He was panicky.

"Slow down," he told himself. He found his jacket, pulled out the glasses, read the instructions on the little piece of paper under the lamp and by the phone and dialed.

By the third ring, he was pacing and cursing. By the fifth, there was a husky, questioning hello.

"Maureen?"

"Yes."

"It's me."

"Hi, me." There was a wonderful, soothing warmth in her voice now.

"I'm sorry to call you this late..." he said, stopping because he had no reason that seemed adequate for a 3:30 A.M. call—not one that he wanted to use anyway.

"You can call me anytime. Are you all right? You sound terrible."

"A little cold, I think." There was a long pause. He realized it was his nickel. "I could not sleep and I just wanted to hear your voice. I'm being really selfish."

"You got a package today from the police. They delivered it. It was stuck inside the door."

"Thanks."

"Besides being a little lonely, I'm all right you know."

"OK."

"Don't worry."

"I won't," he lied.

"Did you have a good dinner?"

"Not really."

"Damn, I wanted to live vicariously. There are a lot of wonderful restaurants in Chicago."

"I goofed. They had pictures of the food."

"See you at the airport at eleven."

Shanahan felt worse the next morning. His head was so clogged he couldn't think. His chest was raw. He looked a little raw, too, when he arrived on the first floor to get the complimentary coffee, a cinnamon roll and a small can of orange juice—the complimentary continental breakfast the clerk had mentioned at check in.

Upstairs, Shanahan never took a second bite of the roll, which had the heft of a bowling ball. He did finish the orange juice and coffee before showering. The hot water felt good. He let it roll over his body much longer than he normally did, eyes closed, trying to focus on getting to the airport, figuring out his dream and trying to piece together the oddities of Barbara Dart's death or disappearance.

If not her, who? A stand-in. If not a crime of passion, why? Greed. It wasn't all that difficult.

He was ready to face the day only because he had to. And he had to because he wanted nothing more than to be home. In his bed.

Downstairs, someone new behind the desk nonetheless told him what the other had said the day before. Because it was raining, Shanahan might have to wait thirty or more minutes for a dispatched taxi. Shanahan would have better luck out on Broadway.

This time, Shanahan got soaked before an empty taxi came by and picked him up.

The Southwest Airlines' gate was crowded. Dozens of young children, many of them romping and yelling and being yelled at in return. Why so many ankle biters? The sign that said the flight was going from Chicago to Indianapolis to Orlando explained it. The Mouse. Damn the Mouse, Shanahan thought. If he ever flew to Florida, he would make sure Orlando wasn't one of the stops. The noise level was irritating. And it didn't help that the television was on and the volume up.

Oprah.

There were only so many places to put your eyes. The frazzled airline rep at the counter, the unwashed, shrill-voiced prepubescent masses, the window out to the bleak tarmac and the TV. Shanahan's gaze was finally drawn to the TV. Long lost daughters met their mothers in tearful, on-air reunions. No, he couldn't watch. He would close his eyes and try not to focus on the volume of liquid being manufactured in his head and in his lungs.

He thought of Melanie and the unsentimental reunion with her father. He thought about Melanie's mother, Hugh's first wife. Where was she now?

Suddenly the alleged lunatic loomed large. Why hadn't he thought about it before? The first Mrs. Dart? Was she alive? It would seem that she might have motive. Where was she at the time of the murder? A great crime. She kills the second Mrs. Dart and sees to it that her husband gets the credit.

Or, the second Mrs. Dart kills the first and leaves the corpse to impersonate the killer.

The first Mrs. Dart was supposed to be crazy. But crazy doesn't eliminate smart.

He still had twenty minutes until boarding. He went to the phone, made a call to Howie Cross, who reluctantly accepted the charges.

"I hope you're not calling from Zanzibar," Cross said when Shanahan got on the line. "Though I have no idea where Zanzibar really is."

"Can you find out from your girlfriend where her mother is?"

"Dead or missing. Isn't that what you're

137

supposed to find out?"

"No, Melanie's real mother, the first Mrs. Dart. There are three Mrs. Darts right now."

"You don't say."

"I do. Is she there?"

"Wait, I'm going to have to finesse this one. Getting Melanie to talk about her past is like getting Clinton to talk about Paula Jones."

"Oh?"

"Yes."

"You've asked?"

"Clinton? No. We keep missing each other at that Renaissance thing."

"No, Melanie."

"About her mother, no. I just assumed."

"I know she's secretive, but I thought maybe she'd open up to you."

"You'd think that, wouldn't you?"

"I'm on my way back. See what you can do."

Maureen ushered a coughing, sneezing Shanahan directly into the bedroom. Tea, a muffin with orange marmalade and TV. He was fortunate enough to catch the Cubs day game. It was a long game and a boring one, affording him long snatches of nap without missing much.

The Cubs had a habit of trading away some of its best talent—Maddux, Palmeiro, Dunston, Grace. It was always a pleasure to watch Grace play. Not a grandstander. Not a guy to swing away at the ivy for a few extra points on his ego, but a consistent athlete who got the ball in play when he was at bat and played solid defense when he was on the field. Shanahan never saw the guy get angry. Just did his job.

Reminded him of a kid on a team when he played in Wisconsin. What a time, Shanahan thought, drifting away from the summer sounds of baseball on TV. Wes Marshall. Outfield. Shock of thick blond hair. Give him a big sky summer day and a field of green and Wes made everything look easy. He remembered vividly an incredibly beautiful day on a diamond in Albion, Wisconsin— a little town with a highway and a general store and a fine baseball diamond. Blue skies.

So strange, Shanahan thought. For a moment, the memory was so vivid he thought he could hear the team taunting the batter. He could feel the sunlight on his face and the wind in his hair. He was awake now. Back in his bungalow in Indianapolis, feeling as if he'd done a little time traveling. Time to get up.

Though an adventurous guide to the city's best restaurants, Maureen's actual, personal, hands-on dabbling in the culinary arts was, at best, minimal.

The evening meal at the kitchen table, which Shanahan managed to attend personally, though groggily, consisted of tea, a toasted muffin with strawberry jam and two poached eggs, bulging eyeballs of some comic character out of Shanahan's hazy childhood.

Jerry Cologna.

"Feed a cold and starve a fever," she said. "I wasn't sure where you fit in."

"I see," he said. "Looks good. It's also encouraging."

"What do you mean?"

"It encourages me to get better."

He decided not to go back to bed, but to read the files his least favorite police lieutenant had sent over. There was a stack of barely readable photocopies. He put on his reading glasses and settled in the larger of the two overstuffed chairs in the living room, a box of tissues on the table beside him and Einstein occupying, no ... owning his lap.

The first report was dated January 15, 1960. The report noted the presence of a female victim in the living room. Initially presumed accident or suicide. Hugh Dart arrived at the scene while the police were still there and was visibly shaken.

The second report was January 17. It noted the fire department's opinion. Arson. The police presumption turned to murder and Hugh Dart was brought in for questioning. So was his ten-year-old daughter, Melanie. Melanie said the two of them had been arguing—that at Mrs. Dart's suggestion, Hugh was to take Melanie to his mother's.

He said he did, said that he did not come back—that he went out for a drive.

Autopsy results showed that the victim suffered a blow to and a bullet to the head.

The next important report was the one noting that there had been a recent insurance policy taken out on Mrs. Dart for the amount of $100,000 with Hugh as beneficiary. Paid double if the death was accidental. Though all the evidence was circumstantial, it was clear that any prosecutor would see that Dart had motive and opportunity.

The fire had obliterated any evidence that might have indicated a break-in. Also because of the fire, no one could tell whether the victim had been robbed.

Now Shanahan wanted the transcript of the trial, though he wasn't sure why. Perhaps new evidence. If he, like the jury, was convinced of Hugh Dart's guilt, he could quit the case in good conscience.

Maureen came into the living room with more tea. She saw the look on his face and returned with a glass half full of J.W. Dant.

The phone rang at eleven. In the bedroom, in the darkness, Maureen answered and strung the cord over herself to get the phone to Shanahan.

"Yeah?" he said hoarsely.

"So I do as you said," came the voice of Howie Cross. "I ask her what her real mother is like."

"Yes," Shanahan said, knowing from the tone that Howie's story wasn't going to have a happy ending.

"So, she gets out of bed. She turns on the light. She dresses, gathers up every stitch of clothing and every goddamn thing that is personal to her and walks out the front door. She says nothing. Nothing at all."

"I ... I ... it's a..."

"My thoughts exactly. I see her face, read her face so well, Shanahan, that I don't say, 'But honey, what'd I say?' I knew. She told me not to ask questions."

"I'm sorry."

"The first non-commercial relationship I've had since I was thirty-two. So what is all this about her mom that freaked her out?"

"Mrs. Dart apparently had a nervous breakdown."

"Good one. Mom number one goes crazy. Mom two is murdered. Dad spends his life in prison and I keep asking questions about her past."

Thirteen

The elderly Mrs. Dart, Hugh's mother, sat across from Shanahan on her ornate blue and gold sofa. Her wheelchair was parked nearby.

"I need to know about Hugh's first wife," Shanahan said.

"She was a sweet woman."

"What happened to her?"

"They were too young to have married when they did. There were so many differences. Temperament. She was a simple woman. A good mother."

"There was a divorce," Shanahan said.

"Yes."

"She didn't fare well after that, I'm told."

"To put it mildly. She snapped." Mrs. Dart gave a prolonged sigh. "She had to be taken away."

"Where is she now?"

"I'm afraid I don't know. We kind of lost track of her. For a while, her mother and I talked to each other—because of Melanie, but they didn't talk about Linda."

"You haven't heard anything from anyone?

Mutual friends?"

Mrs. Dart smiled. "We didn't have any mutual friends. We traveled in vastly different circles, brought together momentarily by the bond between our children. But the phone calls seemed to get farther and farther apart. They seemed less interested in their grandchild. I assumed that Linda had been institutionalized."

"Do you happen to have photographs of Linda? And of Barbara for that matter?"

"Yes. Wedding pictures, I'm sure. Who knows what else."

"Do you think I could borrow them for a while?"

"Why on earth do you need a photograph of Linda?"

"I'd like to find her, talk to her."

Mrs. Dart smiled. "You haven't enough to do to find Barbara's ghost, you need to find and question another woman who has lost her mind?"

"I don't know what to say to that."

"You are truly an ambitious man, Mr. Shanahan. The photos are in the attic. There's a rope in the hallway. That will pull down the steps. A light is at the top of the stairs. There should be an L.S. Ayres hatbox —that was from Linda's wedding. And I believe there is some alligator luggage up there somewhere. Many of Barbara's things are inside."

144

★ ★ ★

It was an older house, possibly built in the fifties, but the attic was spotless. A fresh wood smell remained after all these decades. A little light crept in through the slits of a small vented window at each end of the space. But the main light came from a naked bulb that hung above the opening, turned on by the process of lowering the stairway. Six-foot-wide sheets of plywood ran the length of the space.

This was where Barbara Dart's correspondence had been stored. What else was up here?

Everything was stacked neatly. A floor fan, a stack of cardboard boxes with crayon marks noting "Xmas," more cardboard boxes all neatly sealed, with Hugh's name on them. The L.S. Ayres hatbox was there. So was a complete set of squarish alligator luggage.

Shanahan went for the luggage. He found dresses, shoes, jewelry—all quite handsome. He could remember when people wore the styles. She was a stylish woman. Finally, down to the overnight bag, Shanahan found photos. None of Barbara Dart in childhood. Not one seemed to have existed before the relationship with Hugh. It was as if her life came into being at the wedding.

Shanahan had done this kind of thing many times before—rummaging through the evidence of other people's existence and the debris of their parting. Usually, though, it was all more current. Usually, he'd be sifting through canceled checks, bills and the like—much less personal in some ways, but able to provide direction. How do you get direction from a few static moments—a Thanksgiving, Birthday, Christmas—of the past? What clue could he get to Barbara's whereabouts from something recorded thirty years ago? What could he learn from wedding photographs?

Barbara was beautiful. He put one photo aside to make copies of. He scanned the others. Oddly, he'd met every person in the photographs except the minister, an older man Shanahan guessed was Hugh's father and three women seemingly attached to Hugh's gang—Radiquet, Dickerson and Pritchardt. So, Pritchardt was married. Perhaps still was, though there didn't seem to be any evidence in the apartment. Then again, Shanahan only saw the bathroom, hall and living room.

He put everything back where he had found it and moved to the hatbox, sitting down next to it, feeling and hearing his bones creak. He untied the hatbox. There was a stack of photographs. These were photographs from the Linda Dart era.

He pulled out a photo. A wedding photo, similar to the one he'd selected from the collection of Mrs. Dart number two. He set it aside. There were other photos here. Photographs of Linda with her parents near a lake. Another in the same setting showed a fantastic house up on a long, grassy rise. She was with her father in this one.

More photos showed Hugh and Linda on dates, at parties and then at the wedding. Melanie's baby pictures were here too—a number of them chronicling first walks, birthdays, braces. The photos stopped, understandably, when Melanie was somewhere in the neighborhood of a decade old.

There was the wedding invitation and response card. Mr. and Mrs. Harold Douglas McCullough had issued the invitation for the marriage:

Mr. and Mrs. Harold Douglas McCullough
request the honor of your presence
at the marriage of their daughter
Melinda Anne McCullough
to Hubert William Dart
on Saturday Afternoon, June Twenty-Seventh
Nineteen Hundred and Fifty

Below that it said, "Saint Luke's Church, Meridian Hills, Indianapolis."

Shanahan picked up the wedding photo of Linda, couldn't see it clear enough and put on his glasses. Looked again. If Barbara had the cool, confident, tough beauty of Lana Turner, then Linda had the kind, inexperienced, trusting look of June Allyson—

though, in fact, they looked enough alike to be sisters.

He had become so engrossed in the comparison that he jumped when all the light seemed to be sucked from the attic. He was sitting in darkness. Something moved. A silhouette. It was clear that a human was blocking the light.

"You're a busy fellow." Shanahan recognized Dart's voice. He hadn't heard anyone come up. "Especially for someone who hasn't agreed to take the case."

"I'm not sure there is a case," Shanahan said. "You certainly arrived on cat's feet."

"Didn't mean to scare you."

"Didn't you?"

"What have you got?" Dart moved toward Shanahan, who was still sitting on the floor. The man was still back lit and his features were unseeable.

Shanahan handed him the photograph.

He turned to get light on it. "Mmmmn, Linda. What are you doing with this?"

"Trying to figure out some things."

"Yeah, well, I'm not interested in Linda. I'm trying to locate Barbara."

"You never know what's connected and what isn't."

"What are you trying to say?"

"I'm not trying to say anything. Just what I said."

"You in on this or not?" He moved to one

side and now the light shone on him. His face was rigid. All business. It sounded like an ultimatum.

"On my terms," Shanahan said. "What I'm doing now is investigating you."

Dart flinched.

Shanahan continued. "Inadvertently, I'm also doing pretty much what I need to do to find your wife, if in fact you haven't killed her. If you don't like the way I'm doing this, call someone else."

After a long and disturbing silence, with Hugh Dart's stare bearing down on Shanahan, the man said, "I'll let you know." He handed the photograph back to Shanahan, went toward the stairs.

Shanahan tucked the photographs and invitations inside his shirt, retied the hatbox and got to his feet. He was dizzy for a moment, then got his balance and descended the steps.

He passed Melanie in the hall. She didn't speak. She seemed oddly lifeless. Her eyes were dull. This hadn't been easy. He wanted to say something. But there was nothing to say. Shanahan had been a part of dredging up the nightmarish revelations.

Dart was in the living room, sucking on something that looked like whiskey and water. They didn't speak.

Shanahan couldn't sleep. This was a rare

problem. In his seventy years, he could count the times anything kept him awake for more than half an hour. He slid out of the bed quietly, slipped on a pair of pants and a sweatshirt and went outside. He sat in one of the Adirondack chairs in the dark, with Casey beside him, staring at the silver sliver of moon.

It was cool. As his eyes got used to the dark, he could make out the scraggly apple tree. One of the few branches left was still without leaves. The night was quiet. He could smell the lilac bushes. He heard the muffled sound of a car door shutting somewhere back on the street. Then another. A dog barked. A few minutes later, he heard a train. A soft rumble. All was quiet again.

Then it was as if the sky peeled back to reveal another.

Shanahan was on a rooftop, on his back. Roger—half Collie, half Shepherd—sprawled out by him. He was chilled by the coolness of the spring night. He could see the light of the train in the distance cutting through the rolling farmlands. Lightning bugs flashed below. He heard a voice from inside. "Dietrich." It was soft, inquisitive. The voice belonged to his mother.

Shanahan heard the creak of the screen door.

He was back in his chair. He heard the stretching of the spring. Casey didn't stir.

Had to be Maureen.

A form settled beside him in the second wooden chair.

"I didn't mean to wake you."

"You didn't," Maureen said, laying her hand on his. Her flesh was warm, recently withdrawn from sleep. "I had a bit of a nightmare and I woke up. You weren't there."

"Sorry."

"Tell me. Do you do this often?"

"No. You want to talk about your dream?" he asked her.

"No."

There was a long period of quiet again. Somebody's air conditioner kicked on. Shanahan wondered why. It was a pretty cool night.

"What's up, Shanahan?" she asked, interrupting a blankness in his mind.

"I don't know."

"Has to be something."

"I'm just uneasy. I don't know why. I'm tired. My eyes are tired. My body is tired. But I can't sleep."

He didn't want to tell her about his strange little trips back to his childhood.

"Why don't you just forget the Darts. We don't have to have the income. You're feeling guilty about taking money from him anyway. Maybe that's it. Maybe it's your conscience making you walk the straight and narrow like you always do."

"I haven't taken any money."

"She's either dead or she's vamoosed big time and the trail's awful cold."

"You sound like Howie."

"She could have gone off. From what you say she had no past identity. What's to keep her from making off with a few million and setting up an entirely new life?"

"Nothing."

"Sounds logical. South of France. New York. Rome. Morocco. Tahiti. Bora Bora. Some little town in Washington state or North Carolina."

"I get the point. How can an unsophisticated P.I. without resources find a woman with money who wants to be lost? It's true," he said.

"So what are you doing?"

"I guess I want some answers."

"Like who was her body double?" Maureen asked.

"And why is Melanie not talking? And who is so worried they've got to get rough?"

"We're back to you not liking to be pushed around." She patted his hand. "You're tough."

"A tough old bird. Maybe I've gotten a lot closer than I know. Or I'm much more foolish than I imagine."

Morning. When Shanahan opened his eyes, he found Einstein staring at him. No comment. No nagging for breakfast. Just a steadfast stare that apparently had achieved its purpose. He looked at the clock. A little past seven.

He slipped his legs over quietly so that he wouldn't disturb Maureen, who would sleep perhaps an hour more. He was up. He stepped into the cotton pants that had been strewn across a chair and stepped into slippers to begin the ritual. Something seemed odd. As he passed through the hall and into the living room, there was more light and more cool.

The front door was open. He moved toward what now seemed strangely ominous. He was confused. Locked doors don't blow open. He went to it. It was bright enough for morning.

"Casey!" he called before he saw his dog lying in the dew-damp grass half way between the door and the sidewalk.

"Casey!" he yelled more out of fear than anger. The dog didn't move. He rushed out and kneeled beside the quiet body. A half-pound of red meat was half in the dog's mouth. There seemed to be no rise and fall to the spotted fur.

Shanahan leaned down, head against the dog's side.

Maureen was beside him. Neither spoke until Shanahan raised his head.

"A heartbeat, I think," Shanahan said.

"Please get me the keys to the car, a shirt and my wallet."

Maureen rushed away.

Shanahan lifted Casey, carrying a limp sixty pounds to the beat-up old Chevy Malibu.

Fourteen

Casey had opened his eyes before they had gotten half way to the emergency pet hospital in Nora, a small town now sufficiently suburbanized to be swallowed by the city. It was the only place he knew to go at that hour. Maureen drove. Shanahan sat in the back. As the fear of losing his dog diminished, the anger at the act began to take over. By the time they got there, Casey could actually walk, though he appeared to have spent the night on the town. The vet had little to suggest but that he had been sedated, not exactly poisoned. It was dangerous none the less, the vet said.

At home, the answering machine beeped. The voice was raspy, intentionally disguised, Shanahan thought.

"Could have been you. You got nothin' to gain and everything to lose. Give it up." Click.

Shanahan went to the phone, pushed 69. The phone rang and rang and rang.

Finally a "hello" in a tentative voice.

"Who is this?"

"I don't know who you want, but this is a

155

pay phone."

"Where?" Shanahan asked.

"What?"

"Where is the phone located?"

"The hotel."

"What hotel?"

"The Westin," the voice said.

"Thanks." Shanahan clicked off the phone. Now what would he do? Surely they weren't stupid enough to call from where they were registered. Then again. Could he leave Maureen here?

"Here," he said, pulling his Army .45 from the desk drawer and slipping in a clip. He handed it to Maureen. "Aim it in the general direction and fire. When you pick yourself up off the floor, shoot the other guy."

There was a certain silliness to it all. Shanahan got to the Westin and asked where guests parked. They parked in a vast underground garage where anyone could park. Shoppers, guests of the Hyatt as well as the Westin, visitors to the statehouse and huge Government Center, not to mention the Convention Center. So what if you found an Illinois plate? Chances were, this close to the Indianapolis 500, you'd find several out-of-state plates.

His anger was still festering. There was absolutely nothing he could do about it. He felt helpless. It wasn't just the frustration of finding or not finding Barbara Dart. It was that now he couldn't protect those he loved. And they were in danger because of him.

He emerged from the garage through a different stairway and found himself in the park across from the stately Capitol. That was where the Governor signed bills, shook hands with important people, met the press and where Hugh Dart did his little magic act with the taxpayers' money many years ago.

Shanahan stopped back by Harry's, called Maureen. She was fine, had the .45 in the wheelbarrow as she puttered around the garden.

"We're trying to get some guys together for euchre," Harry said when Shanahan finished his call.

"Yeah. Good," Shanahan said distractedly. He redialed. "Lieutenant Rafferty, please." He waited. Harry said something just as Rafferty's familiar and unpleasant voice came on the phone. "You didn't include the coroner's report."

"You didn't ask for the coroner's report, nimrod. You asked for the police report."

"Should have been in the same file."

"It was."

"I'll pick it up in the morning." He pressed the disconnect button, then dialed another number.

"Cost you a quarter anywhere else," Harry said.

Shanahan put three quarters on the counter.

"Oh damn," Harry said. "Sometimes you really are the hard ass."

"Jennifer Bailey, please," Shanahan said to the male voice that answered: "Bailey & Cornwall."

"She's in conference."

"Have her call me," Shanahan said, then gave him the number of Harry's bar. "My name is Shanahan."

He handed the phone to Harry, who told his friend to pick up his quarters.

"We figure Wednesday nights," Harry said. "Nobody does anything on Wednesday nights. You, me and the other guys."

"Are any of them still alive?"

Harry laughed. "What kind of crack is that?"

"I don't know."

"We can play a couple of tables, Deets. It's what you need. You know Maureen made you tolerable. A night out and you might almost be pleasant. Actually, I was thinkin' maybe you could invite her along."

"Now I get it," Shanahan said. "It's her you want here anyway."

"I wouldn't put it exactly like that."

"Harry?"

"What?"

"You ever get flashbacks?"

"What do you mean?"

"I guess you don't then."

"What the hell are you talking about?"

"Little flashes back to your past. Real vivid. Like you're really there."

"Dreams?"

"No. I don't think so," Shanahan said, now pondering that possibility again. "No," he said more emphatically.

"You know what they say?"

"What does who say?"

"They."

"Oh 'they,' yeah, now I understand."

"They say that right before you die your whole life flashes before your eyes."

"Thanks, Harry."

The phone rang. Harry went toward it. "Sorry."

"It's not my whole life, just little pieces. It's not like my whole life is flashing before my eyes."

"Maybe you're just slower than the average guy," Harry said, picking up the phone. "Harry's? Just a moment." He brought the phone to Shanahan. "It's Jennifer."

"Hello, I need a favor," Shanahan said, taking the phone.

"I think I owe you a few," Jennifer Bailey said. "A legal one?"

Shanahan had helped her niece not long ago. And Jennifer was not the kind to forget. The other thing Shanahan liked about her was that they knew each other well enough that they didn't have to go through the five minutes of social pleasantries that neither of them enjoyed.

"More or less. How hard is it to get the transcript of a trial that occurred more than thirty-five years ago?"

"Possible."

"Would you? And would you read through it and give me an analysis?"

"What kind of analysis?"

"I can't tell you until you've had a chance to come to some conclusions of your own," Shanahan said. "I don't want to put my suspicions into your head."

"Why don't you put those suspicions in my head?" Harry said when the call was over.

"You really figure there's enough room in there? I mean that stew recipe's got your brain packed pretty tight, hasn't it?"

"Quit pickin' on the stew, Deets," Harry said. "Anyway, Delaney's comin' back next Saturday night. That's why I figured we'd play a little euchre, find out how he's doin' and maybe, since it's his original recipe, he can help me finesse that stew into perfection."

"A little 'finesse,' you say?"

"I do."

"I'll see you later."

"Stay a while," Harry said, with an uncharacteristic plea in his voice. "I know you want to get back to Maureen, but you can

160

squeeze in an hour. I'll even buy you a beer."

"I'm impressed. But no." He saw the look on Harry's face. "Harry, a couple of guys came around last night. Poisoned, sedated maybe, Casey. Found him on the front lawn this morning."

"What?"

"They were in the house, Harry. Maureen and me in the bed, oblivious. Maybe in the bedroom."

"Jesus H. Christ!" Harry said, incredulous. "Why in the hell? Why?"

"Delivering a message."

"What can I do?" Harry said. "I can help you do something."

"I don't even know what to do."

Shanahan tried not to sleep. He sat on the chair that gave him a view of back and front. No one could get to the hall without passing by him. Sleep overtook him by five the next morning. Even so, he woke at seven as usual. He felt fine. His neck was sore. His bones ached. But his head was clear. He let Casey out, fed the cat, began the coffee.

He would seek out the McCulloughs. Didn't know if they'd be hard to find. With all that wealth, someone would know. Maybe Radiquet had the guy's name in his little "Who's Who."

The phone book yielded no Harold D. McCulloughs. Shanahan searched the Mc-

Culloughs. There were a number of initials, which is probably what Harold's wife would use if—as was likely—Harold preceded her in death. Shanahan ruled out those initialed McCulloughs in less than affluent suburbs and addresses. That left "N.A. McCullough" on Meridian, a few houses down from the Governor.

He'd wait until nine to make the call.

The voice was tentative, frail. She was the Mrs. McCullough. Her husband was dead twenty years. She had not seen Linda in "quite some time." It was a time she couldn't specify.

"Could it have been shortly after her divorce from Hugh Dart?" Shanahan asked. He would have felt better visiting her in person; however, he wasn't certain a woman who sounded on such uncertain terms with life would allow a stranger to visit.

"I recall her going into the hospital then. I'm trying to recollect whether or not we saw her after that. Seems to me we didn't. It's been so many years. She has not ever faded from my thoughts. Sadly, the details have. We didn't see much of her after the divorce. Of that I'm certain."

"Did you hear from her? Letters? Post-cards?"

"No. It was as if we didn't have a daughter. In some ways we left our daughter in the hospital. She certainly wasn't the same afterward."

"Do you know the name of the hospital?"

"It was in Cleveland."

"You're certain?"

"Yes. I recall what a horrible city it was then. People have told me it's quite nice now. The hospital was very pleasant or we would not have left her there. We found nothing satisfactory here at the time."

"Do you have any idea where she might have gone?"

"I'm terribly sorry. I don't. My husband took care of all that sort of business."

"He didn't tell you anything about your daughter?"

"No."

"I do appreciate your taking the time."

"Why are you trying to find her?"

"Ask her some questions about the time she spent with Hugh."

"Oh, he seemed such a fine young man in the beginning. At the very first we thought she should be marrying someone from our circle of friends. Then we met him and he was a fine young man. Something happened though. We didn't know it was another woman who caused the big change."

"Caused what?" Shanahan asked.

"Why, he treated her terribly. All of a sudden. He crushed her. She believed the sun rose and set on him. Linda would never

163

have understood the way he treated her. I haven't forgiven him."

"Divorces are unpleasant, Mrs. McCullough."

There was a long silence. "I'm going to take leave of you now, if you don't mind. It's all in the past, you know."

She hadn't waited for an answer. He felt rebuked. He replayed his last words in his mind. "Divorces are unpleasant," he had told her. Apparently he hadn't understood just how unpleasant it had been for Linda.

Sometimes this was a rotten business, Shanahan thought, prying into lives, reopening wounds. This was worse. He was unsettling what had taken decades to settle. In a moment, a mere moment, he'd made fresh in an old woman's life her daughter's insanity and disappearance.

He'd had the same effect on Pritchardt too. The good doctor, the learned professor—whatever he was—was visibly disturbed. If Dickerson had been upset by it, he didn't show it. Then again, he was the type who wouldn't show it. And Radiquet? The lawyer seemed to welcome the company, enjoy the memories.

Of course, Linda's mother opened up a can of worms of her own. Where had Linda gone? Was she missing at the same time Barbara was supposed to have been murdered? Had the police checked this possibility?

Fifteen

Shanahan searched through the clutter that had gathered on his desk. Maureen had awakened, showered, dressed, consumed two cups of coffee, pecked Shanahan on the cheek and was out the front door—all with a minimum of conversation. Maureen wasn't always easy in the morning. Especially if she was in a rush.

He picked up the police report. He read through it again. No mention anywhere that the McCulloughs were questioned—not Linda, not her parents. The report was signed by a Lieutenant Matthew Dugger in 1960. There was another officer on the case as well—Sergeant Samuel Washington.

He phoned Lieutenant Swann. He was much too young to have any knowledge of the case, but maybe he knew one or the other of the homicide cops.

"Rafferty mentioned you called," Swann said. His voice, as usual, was neither warm and friendly, nor cold and distant.

"I'm trying to find a couple of cops—Matthew Dugger and Samuel Washington?"

165

"Dugger is easy. Crown Hill Cemetery," Swann said. "Two years ago. I was at the funeral. Washington is retired. I don't know where."

"Working on his tan in Florida?"

"Doubt it. He was plenty tan. Came by it naturally. Wait a minute." A minute passed. When he returned, Swann gave Shanahan an address and a phone number.

"That was quick."

"These phone books. A truly inspired invention."

"I've heard of them," Shanahan said, trying to hide his embarrassment.

"How's Maureen?"

"Very serene about the whole thing."

"No more trouble?"

"No." Shanahan decided not to talk about Casey.

"Be careful. Call me if something comes up."

There was plenty of day ahead for Shanahan and he was having some luck on the phone.

"This is Sam. Leave a number," came the deep, gravelly voice. It was a matter-of-fact voice tinged with warning. The caller better have good reason to call.

Shanahan identified himself, then started to recite his phone number when the same voice came back on—this time for real.

"This is Sam."

166

"My name is Shanahan..."

"Yeah, I got that already."

"Private detective."

"Buying or selling?"

"Asking," Shanahan said.

"Don't need that. Do plenty of that on my own."

"It's about Hugh Dart."

"Convicted."

"A free man."

"Did his time. What's wrong with that?"

"Nothing. Still says he didn't do it."

"C'mon over," the gravelly voice said.

Samuel Washington was a big man, tilting toward 300. But he moved with grace and looked to have whatever fat he carried around securely backed up with muscle. He looked solid. Shanahan figured he'd have to be at least sixty-five if he was a sergeant three and a half decades ago. His mustache and hair showed more than a few strands of white, but he didn't look all that old around the eyes.

He lived on Sherman Drive, a brick home suitable for a family of four, but looking like it was occupied by a large family of one. The living room was dark with black leather sofa, chair and ottoman.

Above the fireplace was a swordfish of pretty decent size and on the fireplace ledge were photos of Sam at various dates and sizes with fish of various species and sizes.

"Thanks for agreeing to see me," Shanahan said. "But why? You didn't seem like the social type on the phone."

"I'm not so bad," he said. "It was a good case. A famous case. Samuel Washington got some good press. It was a good bust. Stood up." Washington paused, smiled. His grim face seemed to explode into humor. "But I always had a strange feeling about it."

"What way?"

"Too much care taken to make sure the body was burnt."

"You express that to anyone?"

"Yep."

"And?"

"And they told me that it was a sign of a passionate murder to want to do that."

"It isn't?"

"Blow to the head. One. A bullet. One. Where was the passion? Don't sound all that passionate to me. Why are you messin' around with this?"

"Dart comes to me. Wants to hire me to find his wife."

Samuel Washington sat down in the big chair and pointed to the sofa for Shanahan.

"Is that what you're doing?"

"I'm thinking about it."

Samuel Washington nodded. "OK. What do you think I have to offer?"

"Did you ever check on the whereabouts of

the first Mrs. Dart?"

"The first...?"

"I can't seem to account for her existence at the time of the murder or after."

"You're pulling my leg?"

"Nope."

"Didn't know about her. Far as we knew that vic was the only Mrs. Dart. What was her name?"

"Barbara. I read the police reports. Not much in them. Not a lot of character stuff. No talking to the neighbors or friends, nothing."

"Didn't need to. Don't know that we got it all on the police report, but there were some pretty damning stuff in the trial. Mr. Dart had a .38. We found a .38 slug in the victim's skull. They had a pretty mean argument. Daughter verifies that on the stand. He had a policy, I think...on her life. He had no alibi. There were no signs of a break-in that we could find. It was his gas can we found. What else?" Washington seemed to be searching for more, then decided it didn't matter that much. "Whole bunch of shit."

"Some people think that this is either some game Hugh is playing or he's crazy and doesn't want to admit to himself that he killed his wife."

"He's spending good money to find her though?"

"To find her or the money she supposedly

169

took when she disappeared."

Samuel Washington smiled again. "Well, now I'd hate it very much if you spoiled my most famous case. On the other hand, you would most certainly relieve me too."

"Why?"

"Cause I have never, ever been wrong when I had the feeling something was wrong. And I felt something was wrong."

"Something else," Shanahan said.

"I'm listening."

"Why would there be a couple of thugs trying to keep me off the case if there wasn't something fishy about it?"

"You gotta point," Washington said. "Something hid nobody wants you to find. Could be her, couldn't it? Someone else who thought it was strange."

"Who?"

"Mrs. Arcadia Jones."

"Who's that?"

"Their housekeeper."

Shanahan rode with Washington, inside the roomy cab of the big black Dodge Ram truck, the driver's seat all the way back to make room for his roomy body. From Sherman Drive to 38th, down Dr. Martin Luther King Street, which was also called Highway 421, and Northwestern, and Michigan Road, depending on how current you kept and what part of the road you were on.

Politics is the art of compromise and confusion.

Crown Hill Cemetery to the left. Golden Hills, a hidden elite community not visible from the street, off to the right. Soon Dr. Martin Luther King Street turned gray and dilapidated. A right turn on Udell Street.

Washington pulled up to a two-story frame house badly in need of paint. Curtains blew out the windows of the upper floors. A couple of the windows on the bottom floor were boarded up with plywood, now as weathered as the siding.

"How are your eyes, Arcadia?" Samuel Washington asked the old woman sitting in near darkness.

"I can see light, so I can see shadows," she said.

"I've brought along a man interested in knowing what you know about something."

As Shanahan's eyes got used to the darkness in the small room of the old, boarded-up building, he saw she was every bit of the ninety-five years Samuel said she was. She was, he thought, old enough to be his mother—twenty-five more years of living.

The house hadn't been condemned. He was sure that the windows had plywood because glass was too expensive.

As his eyes became even more accustomed to the dim light, he saw the large, ornate gold frame on a window sill. In the frame was a young man in an Army uniform. A corporal. Shanahan recognized its vintage: World War II.

"Where did your son serve?" Shanahan asked her.

"Died on some island," she said.

"South Pacific?" Shanahan asked.

"I do believe so."

There was her son, in a uniform similar to one Shanahan had worn in Europe in the same war. The handsome portrait in this elaborate frame, apparently the only thing left of material value for her and she could no longer see it. Perhaps she saw it as a shadow. Hell, the war was only a shadow. Soon, no one would be alive who remembered it.

"This is Mr. Shanahan," Washington continued, "he wants to know more about the Dart family."

There were places to sit. An old, faded, upholstered living-room set—a sofa and two chairs, each with matching fabric and a fringe running across the bottom edges. Washington sank deep into the sofa. Shanahan sat in one of the matching chairs.

"Can I get you something?" she asked them. "Some tea?"

Shanahan started to say "no" but Washington's "yes, please" beat him to the punch.

Arcadia stood slowly, long gnarly fingers

172

wrapping about the knob on a cane. She headed for the other room.

"Just take a minute," she said. "This new tea you brought me, Samuel, is perfectly wonderful. What did you say it was?"

Her diction was more precise than any Shanahan had heard since he was in grade school. He was surprised at the vividness of his memory of Miss Hoover.

"Just Earl Grey, Arcadia. Nothing fancy."

"That her only son?" Shanahan asked.

"She had another. In prison. He won't be back either. Died in prison. She lost them both to war of one kind or other."

"How is it you still know her?" Shanahan asked Washington.

"She had no place to go after the fire. She lived upstairs at the Darts'. I had her stay with me for a short time until she got her affairs in order." He leaned toward Shanahan. "She had some good jobs and some good times between then and now. I've asked her to come stay with me now. But she says it wouldn't be proper, me being single again." He smiled.

"And she never appeared in the police report."

"Nope."

"Nor did Dart's alibi—that he was seeing a prostitute in Terre Haute."

"Well, you got me. I haven't looked at that report for thirty years. But I don't believe

173

anyone told me about any hooker in Terre Haute. I would've checked. And Arcadia? She was in Baton Rouge visiting her sister. She came back the next day. She wasn't there the night it happened. What could she say?"

"A lot."

"Well, you'll just have to ask her."

"Could you help me with the tea, Samuel?"

"Arcadia," Washington said as they settled in again, "Mr. Shanahan would like to know more about the relationship between Hugh Dart and his wife."

"Miss Linda or the one who died?"

"You knew Dart's first wife?"

"Oh my, yes," she said. "I worked for the McCullough family, knew Linda McCullough since the day she came home all fresh and pink from the hospital."

"Do you know where she is now?" Shanahan asked.

"No. The day she went away to the asylum was the day I saw her last."

"You two were close?"

"Yes."

"Has she called you since, or written?" Shanahan continued.

"No, she has not," Arcadia said with a kind of sweet sadness in her voice.

"She had a nervous breakdown is what I'm

174

told," Shanahan said, seeking verification.

"Yes. That is what I understand as well. Samuel, is your tea all right?"

"Perfect."

"And yours, Mr. Shanahan?"

"Very good," he said though it was very strong.

"I have to time the tea now that I don't see very well. Mine seems particularly strong. I could add some hot water."

"That's all right," Samuel said. "I'll get the water if you two want to continue."

It was close in the room. Hard to breathe. And this was only May. He wondered what she'd do in July or August. He glanced at the woman, who stared somewhere in their direction. Shanahan wasn't sure Arcadia wanted to continue; but he pressed on.

"What signs did she exhibit before she was admitted to the asylum?"

"Miss Linda was the kind of girl who could walk through a patch of weeds and see a bouquet of flowers. But in the end she got lost in the brambles. Mr. and Mrs. McCullough tried to create a time and a place that would not interfere with her disposition. As long as she lived at home, everything turned out very well for her."

"And then Barbara?"

"The second Mrs. Dart was always kind to me. And generous. She could walk through a garden of flowers and see every patch of

175

weed. A different woman altogether."

"But the second Mrs. Dart was the reason the first had mental difficulties."

"I wouldn't say that."

"What would you say?"

"In the end, Mr. Dart lost interest."

"In Linda?"

"In both of the ladies. He became a man who looked at them from a long way away."

"Just lost interest? That's all?"

"He had a way about him, Mr. Shanahan. You could be in the room with him and not be there in his eyes. Both of them were so used to his attention. He was the sort of person that when he looked at you, he made you alive. And when he didn't, you weren't anything."

"Hugh did that with Barbara too?"

"Yes. I don't like talking about people, Mr. Shanahan. I believe I've said too much I'll regret."

"Arcadia," Washington intervened. "Mr. Shanahan is trying to find out if Barbara is still alive."

"And the whereabouts of Miss Linda," Shanahan said.

"Goodness," Arcadia said. "Are you a ghost hunter, Mr. Shanahan?"

Mrs. Arcadia Jones had no more news. No more opinions. On the way back, Washington told Shanahan that Arcadia wasn't eligible for social security. She worked until she was in her eighties; but no one she worked for withheld any tax. Nor did she pay any social security tax. So none would come to her. Her husband and her sons had been gone for a long time. She had outlived everyone.

In bed, with Maureen already asleep, Shanahan tried to figure out what he knew and what he didn't know. He knew little more than he did at the beginning—except that two wives were missing. One of those might be dead. If that were the case, which one? Things weren't getting clearer.

Sixteen

Jennifer Bailey had gotten the transcript from Hugh Dart's murder trial. And she had read it.

She called Shanahan at eight.

"I didn't get you up?" she asked.

"I'm up. I'm even alert."

"Good, I've read it and I'm ready to turn it over to you. You want to come down?"

"Sure."

"Offices have moved. I'm at Capital Center."

"Hittin' the big time. Bailey and Cornwall, your secretary said when I called before."

"A partner."

"Davis Cornwall?"

"Yes."

"And you got top billing?" Shanahan asked.

He heard her laugh—something she rarely did. "Pretty good for a black lady, don't you think?"

"Pretty good," Shanahan said.

"Come down this morning if you can. I can break away pretty easily until noon. I'm across from Quayle."

"Big, big time."

"Used to be across from Quayle. He moved to Arizona."

Shanahan punched in Howie's number. After getting a little heat for calling so early, Shanahan was able to create a little inspiration.

"You want me to track down Melanie's mom?" Cross asked.

"Yes."

"You have any idea where to start?" Howie asked.

"Cleveland."

"Cleveland?"

"Mental institutions."

"Good, I can do a little research for my own future. Why Cleveland?"

"That's the last place we know. Could be Catholic."

"Why Catholic?"

"The McCulloughs are Catholic. The wedding was Catholic."

"Brand preference. OK. McCullough. Mental institutions. Catholic. Cleveland. We'll probably learn she's discarded her human container and hopped a flight on a UFO and you'll want me to tell Melanie the news."

The Capital Center was a prestigious address. Downtown. Two identical towers joined by an airy atrium. Outside, having survived the controversy they once caused, the sculpture of two naked and anatomically correct dancers celebrated whatever day it was.

The ride up in the walnut-paneled elevator gave Shanahan twenty-two stories-worth of view of his reflection in brass. The law firm of Bailey and Cornwall was identified by brass letters somehow affixed to the glass office front. Shanahan could see Steve, Jennifer's secretary of many years, piloting a dark, rich desk. Steve smiled when he saw Shanahan, the result of an initial dislike that had turned slowly into respect and friendly recognition.

"Nice digs, don't you think?" he asked.

"You're talking just like her," Shanahan said. The luscious peach upholstery had to be her idea. Not Cornwall's.

"We are nearly one and the same," Steve said, smiling.

Jennifer Bailey came out into the room. Usually intense and severe, Jennifer appeared to have finally accepted success willingly, graciously. She wore it well. She seemed softer, warmer, more relaxed than usual.

"I'm underdressed," Shanahan said. "But that's not unusual."

"Come in, have a seat."

"How's Jasmine?"

"Doing as well as could be expected. I

think she and Luke might be able to pull it off, thanks to you. And thanks for asking. We're building a little history, you and I, aren't we?"

"Seems so."

"Despite the way we started."

"True."

Jennifer picked up a thick file, opened the flap. "Pretty old."

"So's Hugh Dart."

"Who is he to you?"

"Potential client," Shanahan said, glad he wouldn't have to explain how much work he'd done without agreeing to work for the guy.

"I've gone through it. It was fun," she said. "Didn't know I could have fun, did you?"

"I always imagined you could."

"Well, to get a chance to look at Radiquet in his prime. Pretty amazing."

"He was good?"

"No, I meant that I got the chance. Frankly, I wasn't dazzled. It was a little bit of a letdown."

"Tell me."

"Maybe there just wasn't anything to work with," she said.

"Give me your doubts."

"No alibi whatsoever. Out driving. That was never addressed by the defense."

"Supposedly he was with a prostitute in Terre Haute."

"Not much, but better than nothing at all."

"Dart didn't testify in his own defense. Would he have likely made a bad impression?" she asked.

"From the description I get from all of his friends, including Radiquet, Hugh Dart could charm the birds out of the trees."

"So why didn't he testify? There's some other problems too. Listen, what is this all about? Trying to overturn a thirty-five-year-old conviction?"

"Got a minute?"

They talked for nearly an hour. Bailey wasn't too critical. She was, in fact, delighted to read one of Radiquet's cases. Among attorneys, he achieved what most aspire to. He not only excelled in criminal law but also excelled in corporate law.

His clients were usually the big names in town. The politicians, bankers and playboys who got into trouble. If it wasn't the rich and powerful themselves, it was their offspring.

Shanahan told her that she looked radiant as he began his retreat from her office.

She was slow to smile. "Thanks. Life's been good lately. You? Are you happy?"

He pondered it a moment. These weren't things he normally talked about. He was happy, he thought. His life had begun getting better the moment Maureen entered it, ending decades of general indifference and virtual isolation.

"Yes, I am. Glad to see you again."

"Me too. You know Jasmine and Luke ask about you. You helped them through a tough one."

"Tell 'em 'hi.' "

Shanahan walked down Illinois Street, ventured a little farther for a cup of coffee at Hubbard & Cravens. He sat outside with a cup of what the woman described as a Grande Guatemala. It was hot, good. He began to read the transcript himself.

What he read he didn't like. Not only did he find what Jennifer found which made Dart's defense seem weak, but he read the part where Dart's own nickel-plated, snub-nosed .38 was introduced as evidence with forensics testifying that it fired the bullet into the victim's skull.

This was confusing. Dart seemed even more guilty. But Bailey's analysis was correct too. Call it Monday morning quarterbacking, but Radiquet's whole defense seemed to be based on the prosecution not being able to pile the evidence high enough to convict him.

Perhaps Hugh Dart didn't kill his wife after all. If the only reason Dart believed his wife was alive was that the money was gone, then maybe it was her lover, or someone else she knew well enough to tell about the money and Dart's pistol—a lover who didn't want to share.

There was one other possibility. He'd need a little help investigating that avenue.

Radiquet's greeting wasn't quite as warm as it had been the first time.

"I was in the neighborhood," Shanahan said.

Radiquet wore the same suit. There wasn't much change in the papers arranged on his desk. There was the familiar stuffy smell of port and tobacco. A wine glass with the damp residue of red at the bottom was at the corner of the desk. The only change was the open book on the desk, doing the splits face down, in the place Radiquet had put it when Shanahan startled him.

"You've come back for more tales?" He slid his thick glasses down on his nose to look at Shanahan. "I would have thought you suffered enough the last time."

"On the contrary, you spin a good story and I'm interested in the subject. Are you busy?"

"Giving me an out are you? Yes, yes, I'm terribly busy. Didn't you have to paw your way through the clamoring hordes in the waiting room?"

"I didn't see the waiting room."

"Ahh, so that's the reason it's so slow around here."

"I've been reading the transcript of the trial."

"You are diligent, persistent. Sit. If you're going to be a pest, you might at least get comfortable."

"I'm curious about a few things," Shanahan said, rounding the desk and taking the wing-backed chair by the window.

"A little test for my brain and antiquity."

"Tell me why—again—you didn't use the alibi."

"Climate. Moral climate. I'm convinced the jury would have found him to be morally deficient. They would have felt that he possessed so few scruples he would be more than capable of killing someone."

"And why didn't he take the stand?"

"You cannot predict what a man will say in a situation like that. Worse, you cannot predict what he will be asked with total certainty. Sometimes it's not the answers we are worried about, but the questions."

Radiquet's speech was thicker than Shanahan remembered. Yet he had been asked two questions that seemed problematical to Shanahan, and to Bailey, and the attorney shrugged them off as Hercules might brush off a butterfly.

"One more question," Shanahan said. "Seems to me there was no attempt to give the jury other possible explanations for her murder."

"And what might those be?"

"A burglar. A scorned lover."

Radiquet took off his glasses, wiped his eyes with the back of his hand. "In what state are you licensed to practice law? He is alive today because of a good defense. Maybe I didn't free him. But he wasn't strapped in the electric chair, though, was he? He's alive. Isn't he?"

Shanahan stood. "Your little group. Dickerson and Pritchardt. Respectable members of the community, all of them. Why didn't you call them, or anyone as a character witness?"

Radiquet reached into the cabinet by his desk and pulled out a bottle of port. He poured himself a glass, suddenly oblivious to Shanahan's presence.

Why on earth would Radiquet want to lose a case? This was the biggest case to come along. Surely, there was no case he would have rather won. What was all this, anyway? Why couldn't it be what it seemed? Dart killed his wife. Then why were there people who wanted Shanahan and Cross to butt out?

Maybe Dart was using Shanahan as the lamb to trap the tigers. Let the old private eye draw the fire so he could find out who, in fact, took the money.

There was the money, still. Follow the

money. That's what they say, he thought.

"Damn," Shanahan said out loud as he boarded the old elevator headed down from Radiquet's lonely office to the heart of downtown. The boys who roughed up Howie Cross and later visited him had to be clued in somehow. Who knew Howie was on the case, then shortly thereafter, Shanahan? It would explain why Dart was so adamant about having Shanahan and not some more resourceful private investigation agency. "Damn," he said again. And Shanahan was so gullible he wasn't even getting paid to be the patsy. He'd turned down the money.

Dart must be having quite a laugh.

Shanahan's feet had no more than hit the sidewalk than he was reminded of the other twist. Who in the hell could be sure if it was Barbara Dart's body? There had been no comparison of dental records. Fingerprints didn't exist after the fire. How about exhuming the body?

He turned around, went back in. The elevator was still waiting. Radiquet hadn't moved. Shanahan stepped into his office. The attorney was staring ahead, eyes on something, frozen. For some reason Shanahan remembered what he'd been told about chickens. How you could draw a line on the ground and put the chicken's beak on the line. And the chicken would stay there, hypnotized.

"Mr. Radiquet."

No movement.

"Mr. Radiquet!" For a moment Shanahan thought he might be dead.

"Oh," he said, turning. "You still here?"

"I thought about having the body exhumed."

"A little difficult. She was cremated."

"By whose order?"

"Her own. Her will. The court carried out the instructions left in her will." He swiveled around slowly. "So far, Mr. Shanahan, how many windmills have you killed?" Radiquet's smile showed contempt.

Maureen was out in the garden when Shanahan got home. She was planting some small, yellow flowers around the stones she'd gathered and arranged to support the birdbath.

He watched her work as he punched some numbers into the phone.

"Some questions for you," Shanahan said when he got Hugh Dart on the phone.

"Shoot," Dart said, sounding amused.

"Where's Barbara Dart's will?"

"Will? What did she need a will for? She had no family, except me. No belongings except what we had."

"You don't know about a will."

"No, I'd be interested to."

"Who was her lawyer?"

"Far as I know, Radiquet."

188

There was a moment in which neither spoke.

"She did know him, didn't she?"

"Yes. Very well. Liked him. Seemed to trust him."

"And you had him represent you."

"Yes. Because he was my friend too. And because I didn't kill her. Radiquet believed me."

Shanahan wasn't over the idea that Dart was stringing him along for his own purposes, but his case was headed in at least two directions.

He had nothing more to say to Dart. And for once, Dart didn't press him about whether or not he was on the case. Why should he? He was getting the room without paying the rent.

"We have chipmunks," Maureen said, coming in, not letting the wooden screen door crack against the wooden frame. "I filled in one hole, but it seems they've constructed several more."

"I understand the feeling," Shanahan said.

The Cubs were on the West Coast for awhile. San Diego, the Dodgers, the Giants. Maureen made some popcorn for the late-night game, but fell asleep in the seventeenth inning of a Padres game. Shanahan removed the bowl from her grip and set it on the bedside table. He too was drifting. He shut

189

off the television after the San Diego pitcher lined a double down the left field line, stole third and rode home on a passed ball.

The last thing Shanahan remembered before going to sleep that night was Arcadia's haunting question. Was he now a ghost hunter? No, what he did was to right the wrongs so the ghosts could go free. What a thought. Shanahan had never spent much time ruminating about the spirit world. Then again, he'd done a lot in the last few years he hadn't done in the decades before.

The room was so silent, he could hear Maureen's breathing. He began to drift. He could hear the bushes brush up against the window. The wind? Sleep was overtaking him. He heard the sound of two car doors closing. The sound was close. In front, out on the street. At 3 A.M.?

Seventeen

One of the men who got out of the big white Ford Victoria wore a black T-shirt, jeans and tennis shoes. The other wore a black golf shirt and black cotton pants and loafers. In the night the large rounded shapes of their bodies suggested brothers. They moved quietly up on the lawn. The one in jeans checked to see if his 9 mm Glock was still tucked into the back of his belt. The other had his .38 drawn. The long silencer was already attached. He was the one who motioned the other guy to go around back.

"Wait," came a voice from behind them.

They turned back together as if they were part of a chorus line. What they saw was a little white-haired man with a sawed-off, double-barreled shotgun.

"Which one of you is Zorro?" asked the little white-haired man.

"Who the hell are you?" the guy with the big quiet gun said.

"Local gang," Harry said, smiling, motioning his shotgun in a way that suggested they drop their artillery. "The one you got in your pants too," he told the guy.

The two of them looked around.

"Pretty small gang you got here," one of them said.

"Got a round in each barrel. Can't hardly miss from here."

The two guys tossed their weapons gently to the side. "Now your wallets."

"You're shittin' me."

"Come to think of it, I can probably get you both with one shot," Harry said.

They fished out their wallets, tossed them down with the weaponry.

"Can we go now?"

"One more thing," Harry said.

"What?"

"Get undressed."

"What?"

"Take your clothes off. Hurry. If I have to do it, I'll probably have to shoot you first."

They undressed.

"You're a pervert," the big hairy guy said, the one who used to own the silencer.

"Thank you. But you both are way too ugly."

"What now?" one of them asked, seeming a little smaller now that he was naked.

"Get your car keys," Harry told him.

The guy kneeled, rummaged through the pockets of the black cotton pants, found the keys.

"OK, you're free to go."

Harry aimed the shotgun at the window of the car. Harry didn't know who was talking. It was too dark. But he heard one say, "What in the hell was all of that?" The other guy was laughing. "What are you laughing about?"

"You're so fucking macho, I expected you to have a little more going for you."

"Stop looking at it, you weirdo."

"I'm not looking at it."

"You are too."

"Why would I? There's nothing to see."

"Oh shit, what are we gonna do?"

"Drive," Harry said.

The three of them sat in the living room. Shanahan had put on a pot of coffee. Maureen and Harry were laughing as they combed through the wallets for information.

"Not that I'm complaining, but what in the hell were you doing out there anyway?" Shanahan asked Harry.

"Simple. I don't like what they did to Casey. That's not right," Harry said, his humor changing quickly to anger. "He could have died. I wanted to shoot the bastards."

Shanahan brought in the coffee, started looking at the IDs.

Harry, recovering quickly and completely from his explosive outburst, was already embarking on his third telling of the story, embellishing it with drama that might or might not have had some basis in truth.

"Then lightning cracked open the midnight sky," Shanahan interjected. He hated to be the one to bring things back to reality. But what Harry and Maureen were forgetting is that two guys came to the house in the middle of the night armed to the teeth.

"There was no lightning," Harry said in an admonishing tone.

"There will be by next week," Shanahan said. He considered calling the police. At least Lt. Swann. It was the smart thing to do; but he wasn't going to do it.

"Joseph Korowski, Chicago, and Michael McDougall, Des Plaines," Harry said, squinting at the driver's licenses.

"Yeah?" Shanahan said, taking the little plastic-coated cards. He showed them to Maureen.

She nodded. "That's them. But they lied about their height." She smiled.

Nothing obvious came from their scrutiny. Other than the identities and addresses of the thugs, the wallets gave away few other choice pieces of information. Both Korowski and McDougall worked for Woolen Enterprises, Inc., Chicago or at least that would seem to be the case since their gas credit cards bore the corporate name.

"Back to Chicago?" Maureen asked.

He knew what time she left for work. So he appeared on her doorstep at 7:15 A.M.

194

feeling like a twelve-year-old. Howie rubbed his face to check for pimples. None. He was still in that awkward stretch of adulthood between acne and liver spots.

But he wasn't too adult to be nervous, to feel at the mercy of others—as he had during most of his teen years. Intensifying the feeling of powerlessness, Howie was about to ask her father—a convicted felon—if he could talk with Melanie.

Dart, who seemed mildly amused, grinned, shrugged and walked away from the door. Melanie reappeared.

"I just wondered if you could come out and play. I think it's all right with your dad if you promise not to leave the yard."

Melanie swallowed a smile. "A little dodgeball, maybe make some mud pies, some other kind of pretend?"

"I was thinking more along the lines of Doctor."

"Then we wouldn't be pretending, would we? I don't know, Howie. You seem to want to live in the past. My past."

"I do. I still do. Past, present and future."
She shook her head.

"We can't have a whole bunch of hidden things," Howie went on. "Taboo subjects, whole areas of our lives we can't touch."

"Why not? Any law against it?" She stepped out on the porch, sat on the top step.

"I can understand why you don't want to

revisit those days..."

"I doubt it or you wouldn't keep—"

"It's not healthy." He sat down beside her. "I have to ask it. Do you know where your real mother is?"

Struggling to hold onto her composure, she managed only the briefest syllable to escape. "No."

All in all, it still felt like he was twelve and he was stopping by to see his girl and, no matter what he said, he'd be clumsy and make matters worse.

"We need to put some things to rest, don't you think?"

She nodded. It was all she could do, it seemed, to hold back a couple of decades of anguish and confusion.

"Come over, if you want," Howie told her. "I'll be home all afternoon making phone calls. All evening. All night. I'm warning you though. I'm going to be prying a while longer. It's what I do."

"It's what you do," she said, the flatness in her voice indicating personal irony. "We were destined to meet, weren't we?"

Shanahan was already on the phone, running up his personal phone bill. He'd located Woolen, found out that they weren't making sweaters. They were some sort of investment company. For a moment, he thought about getting the head honcho and asking about the two thugs. Stupid, he thought. It also crossed his mind to run Pritchardt's name in front of them. Thought better of it.

Instead he asked for some information about the company.

"I'm interested in talking with someone there; but I'd like to know more about the company. Who are the principals, board of directors, managers, so forth."

"I could mail you our annual report," the woman said.

"That would be great, but I'm in the middle of a decision. I might have to move more quickly. A day or two could mean a significant loss. I'd like to have the information more quickly."

Maureen passed him on the way to the kitchen. She nodded her approval.

"I could fax the more pertinent information," she said.

"Fax?"

"Yes, you have that capability?"

"Oh, of course," he said. "Just a moment. I can never remember our number. I'll have my girl get you the fax number."

"Your girl?" Maureen mouthed with theatrical intensity, coming in from the kitchen carrying a spoonful of what looked to be ice cream.

She grabbed the phone. "This is Mrs. Henderson. You need our fax number?"

Maureen gave the woman the fax number

at the realty office.

"Your girl?" she asked as she flicked the phone off.

"I'm sorry. I didn't have time to think. Actually, it sounds like a rich old sexist, doesn't it?"

"Then again, if you were that rich, maybe I could handle being called 'your girl.'"

The calls weren't going well for Howie. He had stopped at the local yellow pages publisher, borrowed the Cleveland directory, and copied the names and numbers of places listed under "mental health services."

The difficulty was that mental health was big business. Every hospital had some version to offer—sometimes several. And there were others as well. They seemed to be on every corner. Cleveland, like any other major city, was awash with these treatment centers, many with logos of cute bears or seagulls. Many not for the severely impaired—not places where one was committed.

So you had to sort out those which were outpatient services that might be treating tension, mild depression or various contemporary addictions like food, sex, drugs and alcohol.

In the addiction department, Howie was convinced he was batting a thousand.

He wasn't sure which institution did what. Some were called treatment centers, counseling centers, care centers. It was a source of frustration for Howie. What happened to the old days, when they were called "sanitariums, mental institutions or insane asylums," and you could count on the inhabitants being loony?

Perhaps he should have had a little sensitivity training. That was what was being preached these days. It was true, though. Howie often needed some extra couth. At any rate, with all of the names, he was going to find it difficult to track down a patient from thirty-five years ago.

He gave up on that idea and decided to check out some Cleveland psychiatrists. He went back to the publisher, retrieved the book and looked up several Cleveland doctors under the psychiatry heading.

Fortunately, he'd copied down ten names, because the first six he called were either out, with a patient or unwilling to talk. He found a Doctor Roat who was at least open enough and old enough to talk about the institutions that would handle serious cases in 1960. Cross ruled out the public institutions. The private ones weren't all that many. And now Cross had three long shots instead of one impossibility.

Then he remembered Shanahan's remarks about the McCulloughs being Catholic. One of the three fit: St. Francis' Little Shepherd Clinic.

★ ★ ★

Shanahan rode with Maureen to the realty office. It was a small, three-desk office on Tenth. The office was without any living entity save a buzzing fly—a not uncommon condition. The fax, however, was alive and working. And a piece of paper was slip-sliding through the works when they arrived.

There was already a stack in the tray. The woman at Woolen Inc. was competent.

Shanahan thumbed through the papers rapidly. He gave the stack of crinkly, splotchy paper to Maureen.

The board of directors list was alphabetical. He went straight for the Ps and Pritchardt. Nothing even close.

"Do you see Pritchardt's name on the list of officers?" he asked Maureen.

"No."

"Damn. What's the connection?"

Eighteen

"Hi," she said.

"Hi," Howie said, turning from his computer to the entryway.

"You always leave your door open?"

"Not in the winter."

"For someone who got himself beat up pretty bad, you don't think you might be encouraging unfriendly behavior?"

"You can answer that better than I can."

Melanie came into the room, looked around. "I appreciate your coming over this morning. I can be pretty cold, I guess."

"Yeah. You have dinner?"

"I'm not hungry."

"Wine?"

"Maybe."

"A nice inexpensive California Merlot. Guaranteed trendy for at least the next fifteen minutes."

"We better hurry."

"So it's all right if I probe and pry and whatever into your most private life?" he asked, going to the kitchen.

"I think you'd do better after a glass or two

of wine. My resolve will be down. My inhibitions will slip away."

"Then I won't want to waste that time on business." He cut the foil at the top of the bottle, near the cork, slipped in the screw.

"Business, you say? You working for someone?"

"Not exactly."

"See how wrong this is?" Howie asked her afterward. "I don't even find women like you attractive."

"What kind of women?"

"Too perfect."

"I'm not perfect."

"I was just talking about how you look." She smiled. He continued. "Everyone should have a flaw. You should have flabby ... thighs or something. Am I perfect?"

"I don't like hairy chests," she said, running her fingers through the sparse, light blond hair on his chest.

"I don't either."

"We have something in common."

"What we don't have in common is more interesting. I'd like to know things about you that you obviously don't want me to know."

"Did you have a life before you sold out to some guy who wanted you to poke around in other people's lives?" she asked.

"Yes."

"What?"

"Poking around in other people's lives in a more random, more threatening way. I was a cop."

"Why aren't you a cop now? If you'll pardon me, you don't seem horribly successful out here on your own."

"Thanks. I'm not. But I was even less successful as a cop. For some absurd reason I was assigned to vice. And it didn't agree with me."

"What's that supposed to mean?"

"Well, my idea of vice and the law's idea of vice were two different things. I had trouble arresting people for tokin' on a joint and I had trouble with the whole notion of prostitution being illegal."

"Having these high-minded principles, you quit."

"No, having low-minded practices, I was fired. I was discovered with a nickel bag in a brothel. More or less."

"More or less?"

"I was set up."

"Set up?" She clearly didn't believe him.

"I was easily set up, but set up nonetheless."

"Do you still smoke dope?"

"No. But only because it steals away what little ambition I can muster. Actually I do worse. I drink."

"And call girls? Are you still paying for love?"

"I don't know. Am I?"

"Cut it out," she said, putting the pillow over his head. "You dodged the question."

He pushed it away. "I've said a lot. You know I'd tell you anything. I'd tell you my fantasies. What dreadful things I've done in my life. I would tell you my dreams and my fears. You see what's wrong here?"

"No," she said.

"It's the guy who's not supposed to talk. Who isn't vulnerable. Here I am pouring my heart out to you. And you!" He pulled the sheet back, ran a palm over her shoulders, let it slide down her neck and over her breasts. "Just checking. No hair."

"OK. What do you want to know?"

"You ready?"

"Yeah," she said, lying back on the pillow, looking up at the ceiling. "Ready as I'll ever be."

"What happened that night?"

"The night she died?"

"Yes."

"She flipped out."

"Why?"

"She said he was having an affair with another woman."

"Was he?"

"I wouldn't have known. He said he didn't."

"Was he angry?"

"I don't think so. He was calm. Patient."

"You have a clear memory?"

"I remember she had on the mood lights," Melanie said. "She had a way of making the room look glamorous, of making herself look glamorous."

"You remember all that. And you were ten?"

"She was sultry. She was Hollywood. I was infatuated. I adored her."

"You did? You didn't resent her? She took your mother's place."

"Yes, she did. But she was so sophisticated. She seemed that way, anyway. To me. Then. I wouldn't fall for it now. The right lights and our living room was like a set on some movie. She'd have a drink, put on some music. The ice in her glass would tinkle. She'd light a cigarette. Lauren Bacall maybe. Lana Turner, probably. Chesterfield Kings. Those were her cigarettes. I remember because I used to steal one every once in a while. I'd take it down to the basement and smoke it."

"What about your mother?"

"She was a housewife. Then she went crazy."

"That's cold."

"I know."

"You didn't miss her?"

"Yes. But toward the end, she was embarrassing. I didn't know what she was going through. I never saw what led up to her breakdown. I didn't understand it. She turned very strange. Then she went away. She left us. We made it. Miss Arcadia and Dad and me. Then Barbara rolled in. It was exciting."

"What about your grandparents? Your mom's parents. Wouldn't they have wanted to help you?"

"Grandpa had his first heart attack and Grandma, on the best days, couldn't handle dinner, let alone a child. In some ways, mother's crack-up was inevitable. Hereditary."

"Oh?"

"See what you're getting yourself into? Proceed with caution. I could be a psycho like Mom or a criminal like my father. Or both."

"You're not close to your dad?"

"No. I'm not. We don't know each other. I don't know what went on. Did he drive my real mom crazy? Did he murder my step-mom?" She shrugged, lay back, pulled the covers up over her nakedness. "I don't know. One way or another, they all deserted me. I even lost Miss Arcadia."

"So, as one who studied at *Psychology Today*, I've determined you have run very short on trust."

"Yes, it's in short supply. Are you done with the interrogation?"

"Nearly."

She sighed. "What?"

"What happened after she flipped out? That night, I mean."

"Dad took me to his mother's."

"That's it?"

"For the night. For all of it."

"And you believe your father might have done it?"

"Who knows?"

"He was patient and calm and not angry, you said?"

"Yes."

"According to Shanahan, you testified at the trial that they argued."

"Yes."

"But your father didn't raise his voice."

"People can argue without being loud. Someone could drive another someone crazy. Like you."

"Me?"

"You're driving me crazy."

"In a good way?" Howie asked, grinning.

"Not at the moment."

There was a long period of quiet. Howie had turned away.

"Anything wrong?"

"No. Just thinking."

"About what?" she asked. "Past or present or future?"

He turned to her. "A little bit of all of the above."

"Tell me," she said. "And let's be done

with all of this."

"I found your mother today. Your real mother."

Shanahan seemed more shocked at the news than Melanie. Hugh Dart's daughter was sleeping, Howie said on the phone. He related the pertinent details of his conversation with Melanie and the results of his phone calls to Cleveland.

Howie said he wasn't 100 percent sure because there was no ID, but that he had talked to a woman who said she was the former Linda McCullough and the former Linda Dart, that she was happy and living, in fact, in Cleveland with a woman who had been institutionalized at the same time.

"She hasn't bothered to contact her parents or her daughter?" Shanahan asked, setting his fork down.

"She said she was a little ashamed about leaving her daughter, but not about her parents. She said she had worked a lot out while she was away and did not want to come back."

"How did you find her?"

"The hospital had records. The records indicated that the only person she was close to was a Sandy Mazinsky. I called information, found Sandy's number and, lo and behold, Linda answered the phone her very own self."

"If she was hiding, why was she so open?"

"She wasn't hiding. She just uh ... disengaged here and re-engaged there. I explained why I was tracking her down and she seemed surprised at Barbara's death. Then she said, 'As much as I dislike Hugh, he couldn't have killed anybody, not physically.' Her words."

Shanahan went back to his desk, picked up the crinkled faxes. He looked again, determined to find Pritchardt's name somewhere. The list of officers. No Pritchardt, but there was a name Shanahan recognized.

"Jesus," Shanahan said under his breath.

"What?" Maureen asked.

"Samuel Dickerson. Samuel Dickerson, President."

Shanahan would have bet anything that Pritchardt had something to do with it. The man wouldn't look at Shanahan squarely. Perspiration had formed over his lip during mild questioning. He was defensive. Besides that, he had tried to disappear. And he lived in Chicago.

On the other hand, Dickerson wasn't someone you could count out easily. He had a tougher temperament, one at least capable of hiring some thugs to do his dirty work.

Why? That was the question. Why would anyone want to kill Barbara Dart? Why would he?

"Let's look through these again," he said.

Dinner was consumed while they read and re-read the material faxed from Chicago.

"You find anything interesting?" he asked Maureen.

He always gave her more credit than she thought she deserved. Having once worked in a bank didn't a banker make was her thinking.

"Some big money. Real estate. All over the country, it appears," she said, warming to the role anyway.

"Protecting his investments," Shanahan said, remembering the priority Dickerson was giving his life. For his family. How did a guy whose most visible asset in 1960 was a failed Studebaker dealership come up with so much financial power? That wasn't to say he was in the league with a Bill Gates, a Sam Walton or a Perot, even. But he had more clout than the average human. Back to motive ... what possible motive did he have to kill Barbara Dart?

Maybe he wanted to get both Hugh and Barbara out of the way. Maybe the argument had nothing to do with Barbara Dart's death. Maybe it was just the money.

In every new hallway in this strange pursuit, there was more than one set of doors.

Nineteen

Night came none too soon. Shanahan was glad to put off until tomorrow what he couldn't decide today. What to do next. Confront Dickerson? Have another serious talk with Dart about Dickerson? There was good reason now not to trust Dickerson. But Shanahan didn't trust Dart either. Didn't trust Pritchardt, for that matter. It was still difficult for Shanahan to believe Pritchardt was out of the picture.

After the initial discussion with Dart, the ex-con seemed remarkably at ease. He seemed to be sitting back, waiting for the commotion to begin after Shanahan poked at and irritated all the sensitive areas of the case. Where was his passion now? Why wasn't he more engaged in the case himself? Shanahan had anticipated Dart wanting to be more active, demanding to be part of the action and, at minimum, demanding more information on his progress.

This is what he was waiting for, wasn't it?

Then again, thirty-five years in prison must at least teach you patience. Add to that the fact that Dart was a political fixer—a man content to operate from behind the scenes. Perhaps prison had not changed this leopard's spots.

Maureen was in bed, reading. The television was on, but the sound was not.

"If you had a couple of million dollars and wanted to get lost, where would you go?"

"Where would I go?" Maureen repeated the question. She wasn't going to make any snap decisions. "Me? Today. Southern Europe. Warm, good food."

"Why?"

"I'd want to live out a fantasy. Might as well. If you had to get lost, you'd want to be lost some place wonderful! And you said I'd have a lot of money, right? Will you be lost with me?"

"I hope so," he said, pushing a button on the television set and watching Ted Koppel's face squeezed into a narrow bar as the screen darkened and disappeared.

Maureen's eyes trailed back to the book. Face turned into it. Her hair tumbled to hide her face from him. The auburn hair glowed, illumined in the golden light of the lamp on the bedside table.

He placed his .45 under his pillow. He believed the thugs had left, not to return. But he would take no chances.

Einstein was as regular as an alarm. It was

nearly seven when the aging feline walked across Shanahan's chest. The light was gray. He could hear the rain drops against the side of the house. Out from underneath the blanket, the room felt cool. Temperature had dropped. Approaching summer had been hijacked.

Einstein had found a spot near the refrigerator—a bit of heat coming through the vents in the bottom, where the motor, older than the old cat, chugged.

The linoleum floor was cold. And the coolness seemed to seep into Shanahan's bones and make them ache as he walked in the kitchen. He fed the cat. In moments, the tappety tapping sound of the dog's nails on the linoleum alerted the detective to Casey's need to heed the call of nature.

But once the dog felt the first few drops of rain, he turned to come back in. He could hold it longer, apparently. Shanahan hurriedly got the coffee started. Grinding. Filling the coffee maker. Finding the filter.

He went back into the bedroom for the robe and slippers he only wore in the winter. He checked the thermostat and set the temperature back up again to 70—a degree for every year of his life, he mused.

Maureen wouldn't be up for an hour. It was too early to call either Dickerson or Dart. His mind wasn't as clear as it ought to be for such undertakings anyway.

Shanahan sat at his desk just outside the kitchen, where he could hear both the refrigerator and the sounds of the coffee maker. It would be a few minutes before he heard the last gasping gurgle of the coffee-pot. Then the sound of escaping steam. Then silence. The coffee would be done, then. When it was quiet.

It was the smell that had changed. It wasn't coffee.

It had to have been a hot day. The sky was blue. He was with Ed and Tommy behind the barn. The smell was a mixture of hay and cow dung. The three of them sat on a patch of tall green grass, some of it flowering, between the barn and the cornfield. The corn stalks were pale and dry.

It was Tommy's folks' farm. And Tommy had gotten enough Bull Durham tobacco and cigarette papers to make two cigarettes.

"Two pinches," is what Tommy told them. Tommy's older brother would never miss it.

Shanahan was both eager and anxious. He didn't like to do wrong. And he felt like a conspirator. Like he'd stolen the tobacco.

He felt the sun on his head, on his shoulders, mostly on his bare arms. He smelled the tobacco first and Ed inhaled and coughed and the smoke was in the air.

Tommy talked about saving the other cigarette until they met up with the Swensons' youngest. Marie was her name. Both

Shanahan and Ed had a crush on her. If Tommy did, he didn't act like it.

Shanahan could feel the harsh smoke in his throat. He didn't understand why people wanted to do that. He suppressed the urge to cough, but didn't take any more turns. He didn't like the bitter taste it left in his mouth.

He could still taste it.

The coffee pot had grown silent. He heard the thump of the cat jumping from the counter to the floor. Shanahan was back. Where had he gone? Had he been asleep? Had he really gone back?

Shanahan finished his second cup of coffee. He still felt cold and the vision or whatever it was he'd experienced still had him spooked. He went to the bathroom, turned the knob to awaken the bristling shower jets. He waited. The first burst was cold. It would gradually warm.

Was it wise to have a showdown with Dickerson?

What choice did Shanahan have? It was the only thing he had. No, he had Dart. Shanahan looked in the mirror. Dart would dodge as he always did. For better or worse, he'd start with Dart.

The hot spray warmed him immediately. He stayed until he sensed the water starting to cool.

He put on a white shirt, tie. He had a dark-brown jacket and dark-gray pants. For some reason he couldn't fathom, he wanted to look his best.

"Dart?"

"Yeah," came the not quite awake voice of Hugh Dart.

"Why would Dickerson want to beat me up?"

"What?"

"I said why would Samuel Dickerson send some thugs down to beat up Howie Cross and then come to my place in the dark of night wearing black clothes and carrying heavy artillery?"

"Last night?"

"No. The guys who came the other night work for a company in Chicago that Samuel Dickerson runs."

"Yeah?" The voice was bright, hopeful. Downright happy.

"What does that mean?" Shanahan asked.

"I don't know, but we're getting some-where, aren't we, Shanahan? Good work."

"Doesn't make any sense to you?"

"No. But I like it."

"Do you?" Shanahan said. "Could mean he killed her. Could mean he got the money and killed her himself. Be kind of hard to prove at this late date, wouldn't it?"

"You gotta point, but I still like it. Some-thing's happening."

"I'm going to go talk to him."

"I wanna go."

Shanahan's first instinct was to tell Hugh he couldn't go. But almost instantly he decided he liked the idea. He wanted to see the two of them together. He wanted to see what kind of reaction Dickerson would have to his old pal.

Wanting some back up, Shanahan called Howie Cross. No answer. It was early. Maybe he was passed out. Shanahan decided to take his dog instead.

"So neither Pritchardt nor Dickerson contacted you during your thirty-five-year stay at Michigan City?" Shanahan asked the question, breaking the silence while the car wound along Kessler Boulevard.

"I'm not a morning person," Hugh Dart said, dryly.

More quiet. Then quietly: "Nobody visited." He said it flatly. If it was a plea for sympathy, it was perfectly understated. "Oh, except my mother. How 'bout that?" Dart shook his head. Smiled. "Tough guy, right? Well, I guess all tough guys like their moms, isn't that the way it is?"

"You guys have a run-in or something?"

"Nope. Look, it's a fact of life—in political circles anyway. I was a rotten apple. And all the other little apples got as far away as possible. When I was arrested they started climbing out of the barrel fast as they could." He smiled again. His eyes twinkled. He was waking up. "I'd have done the same thing."

"You are remarkably forgiving. Working on a sainthood?"

"That's me. I'm a sweetheart, aren't I?"

"Damned sweet. You say your wife is alive, which means she had to be the one set you up. You say all you want is a little of that money back."

"Christ-like," Dart said. "Is this his neighborhood?" he asked as Shanahan turned off Kessler onto the private street called Sunset Avenue. "I'll be damned. Is he expecting us?"

"I hope not."

"Good."

Twenty

Samuel Dickerson's tanned face turned white at the door, seeing Hugh Dart; but he extended his hand, said it had been a long time and told them to come in—all of them, including the dog. They'd go to his study and Delores would fix some coffee and thaw out some Sara Lee.

The room was huge. Cathedral ceiling. Lots of wood. Skylights. It was all Samuel Dickerson, unless his wife liked the smell of leather and cigars, and shot moose in her spare time.

Dickerson was wearing a bright terra-cotta-colored cardigan sweater over what appeared to be a knit golf shirt of a similar hue. On his desk were photos. Seemed as if Dickerson had three grandchildren, one of whom had created a crayon portrait of Grandpa swinging a golf club on a band of intense green. It was an admirable caricature, one of a guy much too grandfatherly to hang out with bad guys and instigate break-ins and beatings.

There were trophies, mostly golf related

and several framed certificates—honors. One of them was a "Sagamore of the Wabash," a most prized honor, this one signed by former Governor Otis Bowen. Doctor Otis Bowen, one in a line of silver-haired Republican governors.

Kindly, well-respected Samuel Dickerson was doing his best in what had to be an awkward if not dangerous situation.

Dickerson suggested the big leather chairs in front of the fireplace for his two two-legged visitors, while he put some logs on an iron grate. A long match caught immediately and the logs were instantly lapped with flame.

"Remember when starting a fire was an art?" he asked no one in particular. His bald head showed perspiration. The sweat came more from anxiety than the temperature.

There was a huge swordfish over the fireplace—one not quite as large as the one the retired policeman had over his. A couple of heads hung on the tall walls. A moose. A wild boar.

"Delores doesn't like to come in here. Not one for dead animals staring back at her. Don't hunt much anymore, myself."

"Shanahan here is a hunter," Hugh Dart said, looking as relaxed as he did at the restaurant downing steaks and gin. "A man hunter though. Nothing like one of these poor defenseless animals."

"A woman hunter, I hear," Dickerson said, banging back, forcing a smile. He wasn't as cool as Dart, who was warming to Dickerson's discomfort. "Dog's a hunter too."

"I suspect he has some hound in him," Shanahan said.

"You don't know what you've got?" Dickerson asked.

"What do you mean?"

"You've got a Catahoula."

"A what?"

"A Catahoula Leopard Dog."

Hugh Dart laughed. "Sam's got a story about everything."

"You think I'm kiddin'? This here dog is the state dog of Louisiana. Herds hogs, hunts squirrels and raccoons."

Dickerson walked over to Casey, kneeled down. Casey rudely got up, moved around behind Shanahan. He had accepted Hugh Dart easily enough, but it was clear Sam Dickerson wasn't passing the test.

Dart said, "I thought you were going to tell him the dog hunts leopards."

"No, you still think I'm kiddin'. I am not. I've got a dog book around here someplace." He seemed relieved to go looking over the shelves of books that lined the one headless wall.

Delores brought in a tray. Three cups of coffee. Three slices of gooey cinnamon pastry.

Shanahan and Hugh Dart stood.

"You remember Hugh," Sam said to Delores.

"My goodness, yes," she said, shaking his hand. "You are certainly looking well."

"This is Mr. Shanahan. A private detective."

"Is that right?"

"Yes," Shanahan said.

"Looks like Sam is treating you pretty well," Hugh said to Delores.

"I don't have any complaints. He has worked so hard all of his life. He's just now starting to enjoy it." She smiled.

"Delores, would you go see if we shut that outside door?" he asked. She left.

"You really have done well," Hugh said.

"Some hard work, a lot of luck. The love of a good woman."

"Full of shit, as usual," Dart said.

"I'm trying not to be rude, Hugh. But you seem pretty intent on cutting to the chase. So let me help out. What the fuck do you want?"

"That's better," Hugh said.

"I hear some cockamamie story that you're searching for Barbara."

"I may be cockamamie, but the story isn't. I'm trying to find her."

"She's dead."

"I didn't kill her."

"I don't know about that. If you didn't,

then I'm sorry as hell you got stuck for it. But she's dead whether you did it or not."

There was silence.

Shanahan enjoyed watching the movement. Dickerson's aggressive friendliness was becoming an equally aggressive unfriendliness. Then, as if he hadn't wanted to become all that threatening, he continued.

"Listen, Hugh. If you need a small stake to get some sort of business started, maybe I can help out. But hiring detectives and all that—if you'll pardon me, Mr. Shanahan—is pretty low-down and pretty stupid."

"I think Shanahan here," Dart said, standing up and going over by the fire, "was pretty much convinced I was a crackpot too. Like you. But then a couple of things happened. A friend of his gets beat up pretty bad by a couple of goons who want him to butt out of my business. And they go after Shanahan twice. Once they nearly killed the Catahoula Leopard Dog here," Dart said, turning around to face Dickerson.

"I'm sorry. But this isn't a police station. Mr. Shanahan came out here and we talked. And I told him what I had to tell him. That's it. My life's different now, Hugh. I suspect yours is too."

"Very different from yours. That's pretty obvious."

"Is this some sort of shakedown?" Dickerson moved.

"Not unless you got something of mine. No, what we're here for is to talk to you about the two goons from Chicago."

"So?"

"They work for a company you happen to be president of."

"What?"

"Woolen Enterprises, Inc.," Shanahan volunteered.

"Woolen, yes." Dickerson nodded, sat in the chair Dart had vacated earlier. "President. They had to have a name. The CEO runs the place. I've got money in it, but I don't do anything day to day."

"Odd isn't it?" Shanahan said. "You'd be connected like that."

"Yeah. You were connected, Hugh."

"I don't know anything about Woolen Enterprises. What are you trying to do?"

"Woolen bought out McCormick & McCormick. Remember?"

Dart seemed confused for a moment. You could see the truth dawn on him. But the sudden enlightenment gave way to new confusion.

"I cashed that all in to pay my attorney's fees. I don't have anything to do with those folks."

"Well, maybe you pissed somebody off up there," Dickerson said.

"Pritchardt had some stock in McCormick & McCormick, didn't he?" Dart asked.

"I don't know. I wasn't that fucking close to Pritchardt." Dickerson shook his head. "It doesn't take you more than a few seconds to work me up like you did in the old days."

"Doesn't take much to make you sweat. Just like the old days."

The ten minutes that transpired before Shanahan and company departed felt more like a half a day. Every subject seemed to possess its share of land mines and Dickerson wanted to avoid them as much as Hugh Dart wanted to set them off.

"I have some people to see and some things to do," Dickerson said when finally he'd had enough. His demeanor had grown a little harder by that time. He didn't restate his willingness to loan Dart some money. He didn't even wish his former friend well. At the door, he nodded toward Shanahan.

"Nice dog you got there, Mr. Shanahan. Take care of him, eh?" Dickerson's face was stone.

Dickerson as prime suspect faded slightly. Although Shanahan couldn't be sure there wasn't some kind of threat veiled in Dickerson's suggestion that Shanahan "take care" of Casey.

Suspicion now favored Shanahan's earlier target, Pritchardt. The doctor was still in the running. But what bothered Shanahan even more was that there was a connection—

225

however dated—between Hugh Dart and the company the thugs worked for.

Shanahan said little more than he had to while he drove Dart back to Melanie's.

"Something's fishy, don't you think?" Dart asked.

Shanahan nodded.

"She would have wanted help," Dart suggested.

"Or one of these guys killed her."

"No." Dart was certain. "No one killed her."

"How do you know."

"I know her."

"What you're saying is that Barbara isn't the kind of person to die. I haven't met that kind of person yet."

"Well, maybe you'll get the opportunity."

At home, Maureen was getting ready. She was showing a house at noon.

"You know that Casey here is no ordinary dog," Shanahan said.

"I never thought he was ordinary."

"No, I mean he is not a mongrel. Not a mutt."

"No?" she said, grinning, unbuttoning then rebuttoning the next to the top button of her white blouse.

"I like it better buttoned."

"No, you don't."

"When you go out, I do."

226

"So what's this about Casey?"

Casey's eyes opened and he wagged his tail in a motion similar to those of helicopter blades.

"He is, if Samuel Dickerson is to be believed, a Catahoula Leopard Dog."

"My, my," Maureen said, petting Casey. "You hunt leopards, do you?"

"Haven't had any leopards around here since he showed up," Shanahan said.

"Is this true?" she asked.

"I don't know. Dickerson is full of it. And he wanted to talk about something other than what we came to talk about and to someone else other than Hugh Dart."

"Hmmmmmn, interesting."

"You have a hot client?" Shanahan asked, noticing that she looked particularly attractive for her appointment.

"Don't know yet. But since I listed the house I get a nice little chunk if I also sell it."

"Second showing?" he asked.

"First, but she knew a lot about it."

"She?"

"Yeah. She. Now you want to come along?"

"Something like that."

Twenty-One

The house was empty.

Sometimes Maureen felt a little uneasy meeting strangers at homes, particularly empty ones like this one, set so far off the street. If it hadn't been so early on a bright day, she would have waited in her car outside on the street until the potential buyer showed.

But it was sunny. The house was fascinating—one of those beautiful, old and large homes on the parkway, way up on a hill, sheltered by a healthy growth of evergreens and budding ivy.

She hadn't seen the home since the owners vacated. And she wanted to have a closer look, perhaps do a little fantasizing. It was a great neighborhood and she had already thought about how maybe she and Shanahan could live in this house. The home they lived in was full of Shanahan's history. She wanted a home they could share. This was perfect. The same side of town.

Maureen waited by the door for a few more minutes. But she was too curious to wait for her prospects.

The hardwood floor echoed her footsteps in the high-ceilinged living room as she began her personal tour. Large, handsome fireplace. Tall windows. With her income and Shanahan's social security—not counting the occasional dollars from investigations—they could pull it off. She went down the hall to the kitchen. She wanted to look at the backyard. There was the dog to consider. There was the gardening. What kind of sun would it get?

The kitchen was bright, as was the portion of the backyard she could see from the window over the sink. Good space and plenty of it for a garden. What the owners had done, though minimal, was pleasant.

Being a few minutes early also gave Maureen a chance to build her confidence, think about the selling points. Walk around the house, get familiar again. It seemed different from the look it had had when she'd listed it. The Farbers' furniture was still there then. The Farbers' character imposed itself upon all the rooms. There were even Farber smells. No more. The house had the smell of old paper. Not a bad scent. The walls no longer showed family photographs. Little sayings like "too soon old, too late smart" were gone and the house now seemed richer. It was more charming empty than it was with the Farbers' imprint.

Maureen had never been to England, but somehow the house felt English.

She would check out the second floor and the basement; but perhaps she should lock the front door first. The hardwood floor squeaked beneath her as she passed through the dining room.

A man stood just inside the front door. Tall. A broad frame, yet skeletal as were the features on his face. One side of his neck showed what seemed to be remnants of a severe burn.

"Yes?" Maureen said, trying not to show how much she had been startled.

The man said nothing. Then she noticed the other man. Shorter, stouter. Well-tanned. He was standing to the side. In a shadow by the fireplace.

"Nice place," the tanned man said.

"Yes. I was expecting a Miss Blanchard."

"Well, she won't be coming."

"Oh?"

"I wanted to take a look for myself."

"And you are...?" she asked him, eyes darting back to the tall man, who remained quiet. Deadly so, it seemed.

"Jack."

"Jack who?"

"Jack's good enough for now."

"Is this what you're looking for?" Maureen asked.

"Oh yes. Precisely."

"Yes?"

"Very private. Back away from things," he said, smiling. "Quiet. Neighbors can't see in. Probably can't hear anything either. You know, that kind of thing."

"The two of you?" she asked, letting a little inhospitality creep into her voice.

The tanned man smiled, turned to the tall quiet guy with the narrow eyes.

"What do you think?" he asked the guy. "You want to move in here with me?" The guy said nothing. "I don't think so."

"Why don't you two look around? Go upstairs, the basement."

"Might have some questions. You coming along?"

"I'm expecting some other people any minute now," Maureen said. "I should wait here by the door. But do go ahead. Make yourself at home." She started for the door.

"Pretty remarkable woman, Maureen." The tall man edged toward the door and the tanned man moved toward her. "You know, what a mean world we live in. Coming here by yourself." He looked around, eyebrows lifted. "All alone here in this empty place. Things could happen."

"Yeah, well, like I said, I'm expecting others. So it's pretty safe."

She felt as if she'd been punched in the stomach. She could feel her heart racing. For a moment, she thought the fast and heavy

231

beat was making her shake. But the shaking was all inside. It seemed to take all of her energy just to stand there. Her legs seemed to be without muscle.

There was a muffled electronic sound coming from the tanned guy's coat. He reached in his pocket, pulled out a small cellular phone. Flipped it open.

"Yeah, you rang?" There was a pause. His gaze went from the floor where it had wandered when he answered the phone up to Maureen. "Really. I'll be damned." His lips formed a thin smile. "OK. Makes no difference to me."

He flipped the phone shut, put it back in his coat pocket.

"Funny how things happen," he said to Maureen. "You just damned never know. Anything can happen at any time." He turned back to his partner. "We're outta here."

The tall quiet friend nodded.

There was a knock on the storm door.

The tall quiet guy turned to see, then turned back to the tanned guy.

The door opened. It was Shanahan.

"Mr. Phelps," Maureen said. Shanahan glanced around. The two guys smiled. Maureen continued, "I'm glad you came back in the day time. You really didn't get to see much of the outdoors. Let me show you the garden. Excuse us," she said, taking

Shanahan by the elbow and ushering him through the two and out the front door.

"Don't go in there. Let's go," she said.

Shanahan halted momentarily. He knew something was wrong. Drastically wrong. He started in. Maureen caught his arm again. There would be no stopping him.

"Get in the car and get out of here," he told her, breaking away.

Inside, no one. Nothing. It was as if no one had been there.

"It all happened so quickly, I didn't record much," Shanahan told Maureen as the two of them sat at Harry's bar.

"How come you came along when you did? You checking up on me?"

"Constantly," Shanahan said.

"No, really."

"Really. Just didn't like the idea of you meetin' up with strangers."

"I do it all the time."

"Well, now's definitely a bad time for that sort of thing."

"The tall guy was just freaky. Never said a word. The other guy looked harmless, but his words weren't."

"He was tan, wasn't he?"

"Very," Maureen said. "And he wore a summer suit. His shoes were like woven, sort of dressy, but sort of open. Real summer."

"Not from here," Shanahan said. "Not

from Chicago either. Not in April. No time to get a tan like that up there. Big cast of characters."

"What do you mean?"

"I mean these two guys aren't the same two guys as before, right?"

"Right?"

"The cast is getting bigger. This isn't over Barbara Dart not wanting to be found. This is about money. No piddling amount either."

Harry cleared his voice and began wiping the bar in front of them.

"Use your phone, Harry?"

"So now you're askin'?" Harry sensed Shanahan's mood. "Yeah, sure. Of course." He brought the phone over to his friend, the cord stretching across the space between bar and back bar. Harry looked up at the television.

"We have to talk," Shanahan said into the phone after a few moments. There was a brief pause. "Now."

Sinatra was singing. He had done it his way. There was a black and white movie on TV. Ingrid Bergman. Cary Grant. Maureen was watching. Harry was leaning against the bar, talking to McGinty, a regular.

Shanahan had just downed a shot of J.W. Dant and followed it with a Miller High Life chaser when the door opened. It must have cooled down a bit. Hugh Dart was wearing an overcoat. He looked around the bar as he approached Shanahan. His face was grim.

"Whatdya got?" he asked Shanahan. The voice was monotone. He seemed almost bored.

"Another pair of enforcers," Shanahan said.

"Yeah?" Hugh Dart sat on the stool next to Shanahan. Harry started over; but Dart waved him away.

"More threats," Shanahan said.

"Comes with the territory, doesn't it?"

"It does."

"So?"

"Different goons," Shanahan said, closely watching Dart's face for a sign of something. Interest. Concern maybe. Amusement even. Nothing. Dart could have been holding a pair of threes or four kings.

Dart pulled a check book from the inside pocket of his overcoat.

"Don't worry about it. We're done."

Shanahan was going to tell Dart the same thing. Nothing was worth Maureen—or his dog—getting hurt. "You're calling it off?"

"That's what you want, isn't it?"

"I guess," Shanahan said, tentatively.

"It's what I want, too. So we agree."

"After all that to-do over getting me to work on this for you?"

"Yeah."

Dart started writing.

"This was never about finding your wife, was it?"

Dart shrugged.

"Did you get what you wanted?"

"I can take it over, now," Dart said. His look was hard. "I appreciate what you did."

"What did I do?"

"What I wanted you to?"

"Stir the pot."

Dart looked up. He wore a thin grin. "Yeah. That's as good a way of puttin' it as any."

"So you duped me?"

Dart shrugged.

"You kill her?"

"Law says I did." He ripped off the check and laid it face down on the bar.

"That's hardly a confession."

"You know what a good lawyer will tell you? He'll tell you that when you confess you lose your options."

"Thanks for the free advice."

"No. Thank you. I mean it. Sorry if it looks to you like I took you in. I mean it. You're a nice guy. I like you. Sorry it got rough, too. You're better out of it now anyway, while you're safe and still have a clear conscience. Don't worry. It'll all be OK now. I'm sure."

Twenty-Two

Shanahan was surprised and a little miffed that he'd been dismissed from the case. It didn't matter that he was going to withdraw from it on his own.

"So what's going on in that pretty little head of yours?" Maureen asked, grinning. Dart had been gone about five minutes, leaving Shanahan quiet, almost sullen.

"I was about to tell him to take this job and shove it," Shanahan said, folding the check in half and putting it in his shirt pocket, "but now that I'm fired..."

"You're going to step up the investigation."

"Another trip to Chicago. You want to go?"

"Yeah."

"We'll drive up."

"Stay the night?"

"Maybe. What I have to do won't take that long."

"Eat though," she said. "We have to eat."

"Well, I suppose," he said. "We'll stop at a McDonald's or something," he said not looking at her, not wanting her to see he was teasing.

"Yeah, right. McDonald's," she said. "That's about as likely as you ordering a frozen daiquiri."

"Hey, Harry. One frozen daiquiri."

"What in the hell did you just say?" Harry said.

"I figure this trip is going to set you back some," Maureen said. "Hope that check was big enough to cover a really good dinner."

"Hey, Harry. I said I wanted a daiquiri. Open your little bartender's cheat book if you have to."

"Next thing, you'll be wantin' to bring in ferns," Harry said.

"And palms. And video games."

The intent was to drop Maureen off somewhere on Michigan Avenue where she could shop while Shanahan confronted Pritchardt again. He seemed the far more likely of the two—Pritchardt and Dickerson—to break. Maybe there was a way to get the two of them at each other so that the whole thing, whatever it was, would unravel.

Shanahan left Casey and Einstein with Harry. Einstein was content in the back room. Casey found a cool corner in the bar. Fortunately, Harry wasn't a stickler for health code violations—at least when it came to animals. If they had some means to pay for their drinks, they'd be seated at the bar.

As far as the house went, anyone who wanted to break into it, could. There would be nothing of any great value for anyone to harm. The thugs were welcome to all they could carry.

Visually, the drive was boring. There was a flatness to the farmland plains across Indiana and Illinois and much of Iowa at this latitude and longitude. Crops were barely in. Mostly corn and soybeans. But they were only faint lines of green in the land that had so many straight rows, the ground could've been covered with corduroy.

The conversation was, by turns, focused on food, the Dart puzzle, food, the possibility of moving into a larger home, and food.

They got into Chicago a little past 3 P.M. Both were quiet as Shanahan threaded the traffic on busy, unfamiliar streets. Finally, Shanahan pulled over by a line of taxis in front of Water Tower.

"Be out here on the corner at seven. Find some place down here for dinner. We'll do it right," he said.

She would have none of it.

"The dinner, yes. But the little woman does not want to stay behind and shop all afternoon."

"You're not such a little woman," he said.

"You're walking an awful thin line there, partner."

"Thin, you say?"

"Stop it. I can go with you. This isn't the OK Corral, you know."

"Frightened people are more frightening than those who aren't frightened, because they are frightened and they do stupid things."

"I have no idea what you just said. But, I want to go."

"A lot of it is waiting. I'm not sure when he's going to be home. He's teaching, so he could be home now. Or he could be awhile. Or he could be visiting his Aunt Edna in Peoria and may not be home for days."

"I can wait with you. Unless you don't like having me around." She smiled. She knew she had him.

Unlike his previous visit, the door at the entrance was closed, locked.

"You going to buzz him first?" Maureen asked.

"I don't think he wants to see me."

"How about me?"

"My guess is he doesn't like people very much."

Maureen pushed a button at random. No response. Another. A woman's voice was recognizable through the static. "Yes?"

"This is Marjorie," Maureen said, "I clean 309, and I left the building key in my other purse. Could you let me in?"

"309?" the voice said.

"Yes." Maureen read the name that was beside the buzzer—J. and R. Marquette. "The Marquettes," she said.

"Sure honey," the voice said. The buzz.

"You're good," Shanahan said.

"I didn't know you did this," Maureen said as Shanahan produced a couple of metal objects—a tension wrench and a diamond-headed pick, he called them.

"I knocked first," Shanahan said, inserting the top of the 3-inch wrench into the lock, followed by the skinny pick.

"This is illegal," she said, more as an acknowledgment than an allegation.

"Yes."

"Why don't you use a charge card?"

"Not on these old locks," Shanahan said.

"It's taking you longer than it does those guys on TV."

"They have to hurry up for the next commercial."

"Oh."

At least three minutes, maybe more, went by before Shanahan felt the lock give. He turned the handle and pushed in.

"Please stay out here for just a minute, OK?"

She raised an eyebrow.

"Please," he reiterated.

She sighed a reluctant agreement.

Shanahan went in. It was cool. Someone had the heat down around 60, he'd guess. It was quiet. The place was as he remembered it. He moved briefly into each room, checked the kitchen, then the bathrooms, behind the curtains.

He wasn't so much fearful that Pritchardt was in hiding, but that maybe he was dead. No telling what an unstable guy like Pritchardt might do if he felt the world closing in on him. He went back to the door and let Maureen in.

"It's cold in here," she said.

"Maybe he's been gone awhile or maybe he likes to conserve energy."

"Good taste in food," Maureen said, from the kitchen.

"You're getting right into this."

"What are we looking for?"

"We're not looking for cookies, Maureen, so the kitchen may yield few secrets."

"All right smarty pants," she said. "How about this?" She called him from the small room off the kitchen, once intended as a dining room, but one that Pritchardt used as his office.

She had moved to the desk. A small, handsome Rolodex file was open and the card showing was the Faherty Travel Agency.

"I'm impressed. Could be that Pritchardt went on a little trip. Now the question is, is it one that was planned? Or one motivated by some sudden knowledge?"

"Did Hugh Dart make a phone call?" Maureen asked.

"How would he have gotten the number? Remember how you had to get it."

"Maybe Dickerson called him."

"Yeah. But Sam Dickerson acted as if the two of them hadn't talked in years."

Shanahan went back into the bathroom off the main bedroom. Looked as if the toothpaste and toothbrush and other essential toiletries were gone.

"He's made a trip."

"Where?"

"Let's call the travel agency."

"You want me to do it?" Maureen asked.

"No. Two can play at this game."

Shanahan sat at the desk, picked up the phone and punched in the numbers.

"This is Augustus Pritchardt's dad, Morris."

"Yes, Mr. Pritchardt."

"Well, Augie has gone off and forgot to tell me where he was staying. Well, he always does. But this time, I was hoping maybe you could tell me what hotel you booked him into? He's tried so often to get me to use you guys that fortunately I remembered your name."

"I don't know if I should ... um..." came the troubled voice back.

"Well, ordinarily it wouldn't be any big

deal. Just that they moved the operation forward and I know he'd want to know..."

"Oh dear," the voice said.

"Well, it's not that big of an operation. Bypass surgeries are done every day now."

"Listen. Let me check with Gwendolyn. I think she was the one working with Mr. Pritchardt."

Maureen shook her head. "I didn't know you did that sort of thing. This puts everything into a whole new perspective."

"You're not supposed to watch how they make laws or sausage either," he said, palm cupped over the phone.

He opened the desk. Nothing in the middle drawer. He was rummaging through the side drawers, finally thumbing through the papers in the lower, file drawer, when Gwendolyn came on, introducing herself.

"He's staying at the Delano, Mr. Pritchardt."

"Oh, thank you," Shanahan said, trying to think if he knew where the Delano was. Couldn't. "That's not in Phoenix, is it?"

"No, no. Miami."

"Oh yes, that's right. He was going to go to Phoenix, then decided against it. Thank you," hanging up quickly.

He found the file he was looking for. It was still labeled McCormick.

There were check stubs. Several of them. For very significant amounts. It was clear that unless Pritchardt had some heavy and expensive habits, he didn't have to teach for a living.

"So where is he?" Maureen asked.

"Miami."

"Hmmmnn," she said. "A beach, some sun. Great food. I think I'll become a private eye. It has selling real estate beat all to hell."

"You forget I no longer have a paying client."

All of the Chicago restaurants Maureen had read about were booked. They struck out on their own and found a little place not too far from the river. Mambo Mama's. Cuban food.

"Just practicing," she said, over a plate of chicken, rice, beans and fried plantains. "Great Cuban food in Miami, I hear."

Twenty-Three

The Cuban food turned out to be a prelude to the next trip. When they returned home from Chicago, Maureen made reservations for the flight.

Shanahan, interested but uneasy about being on unfamiliar turf alone, called Howie Cross. He gave the young detective some specific instructions.

Maureen continued the arrangements. Reservations at the Delano, where Pritchardt was staying, were out of the question. Booked. But she learned that the hotel was in South Beach. The area wasn't large, so she made reservations nearby.

Shanahan called Cross again, providing an update to the plans.

The Art Deco Hotel and Golf Club had the only rooms available. Shanahan imagined some resort hotel overlooking guys in white caps strolling, sticks in hand, over the rolling green manicured lawns. Some place generally quiet, catering to the Sam Dickersons of the world.

Perhaps it could have been farther from

the truth. But it was far enough. Gladly. The cab driver had trouble finding the hotel that the address indicated was right on Ocean Drive—the main drag of which appeared to be at this evening arrival a glittering haven for the young, the beautiful and the barely dressed.

The hotel was situated in a two-story building over two shops. The sign, almost invisible among all the neon, signaled a side gate entry. There was a narrow walk between the building and a sidewalk café that led to an elevator. The lobby—and the entire tiny ten-room hotel, for that matter—was on the second floor.

An attractive woman with a foreign accent checked them in. Shanahan looked around for some indication of golf. The lobby of the Art Deco Hotel and Golf Club suggested nothing of golf. No photographs of great golf courses of the world. No LeRoy Neiman prints. Nothing.

They had a large, pleasant room with a big picture window that overlooked the ongoing celebration on Ocean Drive. There was a view of the beach and ocean beyond. Palm trees waved from the sand, the palm fronds' feathery shadows barely lit from the lights of stores, clubs and restaurants that lined the drive.

It was eleven before Maureen and Shanahan had cleaned up and hit Ocean Drive.

The crowd had swollen since their arrival. There was a buzz on the streets, the kind of electricity you feel during fairs and festivals.

Shanahan looked around. He really didn't want to run into Pritchardt yet. Or the goons. He also wanted to put that out of his mind tonight anyway. Maureen looked happy. Radiant. Despite the fact that he felt overdressed and overaged and very Midwestern, he felt good. It was Maureen, no doubt. She gave off an aura of energy that was contagious.

The lady with the accent sent them down to the News Café if all they wanted was a quick bite. It was good advice. Shanahan had an omelette and Maureen a sandwich as they sat looking outside at the exotic parade of passersby.

"What's the plan?" Maureen asked after about ten minutes of eating and absorbing the atmosphere.

"I'm not sure. But I think I know what I'm doing."

They walked along the beach. The air, the ocean, the line of Deco hotels across the drive gave him an odd feeling, the same feeling he had during those moments when his youth invaded these older years. It was as if all time was interchangeable.

Shanahan had experienced another strange bout with time on the plane. For a moment, he was in his dad's truck—a Model A Ford reworked with a truck bed. His red dog, mouth open, panting in the breeze as they headed along the Wisconsin highway from Albion to Janesville.

A moment, that's all it was. A flash with surround-vision and surround-sound and the noon light of what had to be the 1930s and the smell of fertilizer and farmland.

He thought about mentioning it to Maureen. But maybe these visions, or this leakage of time was craziness, the beginnings of dementia and him telling her would be the mad rants of an old man. He didn't want to worry her. He didn't want to worry himself.

"What are you thinking?" he asked her, to stop his thoughts in their tracks.

"How wonderful we are, you and I," she said. She laughed. "And everybody else."

Shadows moved near the tide line. Bodies in blankets rolling on the sand.

He was startled for a moment. He was more aware now, it seemed, of the arbitrary world—one where death, injury, terror would come without warning. And they would come from unexpected places. Maureen hadn't been startled.

"Love, passion..." she said.

Shanahan and Maureen moved on by them. Sounds of people on the street in the distance. An occasional car horn. Sometimes the lights from the cars flashed out briefly on the sand.

"We are, aren't we?" Shanahan said.

Morning brought with it some amount of dread. There would be some sort of confrontation, Shanahan thought. Whatever was going on, was going on down here. Maybe it should be a police affair. But he had nothing to give to them. In fact, he wasn't sure he'd recognize what was going on if he saw it.

All he knew was that he had been looking into something someone didn't want him to see. He figured someone had played him. Dart for one. Now he wanted to know what it was and he was ready to let the chips fall where they may—as long as they didn't fall on Maureen, of course.

He had a plan.

He asked Maureen to make some calls. One was to a limousine service. He didn't want a stretch or anything eyecatching, but he wanted something nice enough to get him into the better neighborhoods.

She arranged a Lincoln Towne Car and driver for ten that morning. Shanahan got into the car—leaving Maureen behind to take care of another part of the plan—and told the driver to go to the Delano.

At 10:30 Maureen was to call Pritchardt's number again. She was asked to say, "Come over now," then hang up.

It didn't take long to get there. The driver,

a young sturdy Cuban who warmed to Shanahan's unconventional requests when presented with a fifty dollar bill, waited in the semicircular drive in front of the hotel as Shanahan went in.

He hadn't seen very many hotels like this. A very dramatic entry hall, drapery that seemed about three stories high. He walked back, through the hotel, searching for other ways out. He got to the back, went through a restaurant and out the back door to the pool. The sunlight was dappled by rows of tall palms. A beautiful place.

Shanahan scanned the area for signs of Pritchardt. He walked down by the pool, completely lined by mostly bare chaise lounges, all with towels and elegantly ready for guests. Shanahan kept going. There was a maze of chaise lounges just inside a fence that separated hotel property from the beach. This space was reserved for obvious sun worshipers. Most of the chaises were occupied—all by tanned, oiled and in-shape male bodies wearing nearly identical swimsuits. The bodies all looked so similar, they looked like they'd been assembled using the same well-designed, mass-produced parts.

There was a back gate that led out to the beach. No other exit from the back that he saw. He looked at his watch. 10:15. He had fifteen minutes to kill. He wandered back through the grounds and noticed people wandering out into the pool area. There were some elderly couples. A family. Bright-eyed, pretty blond children drinking orange juice. Waiters brought exotic-looking drinks to the others. Pampering was in the air.

Shanahan had worried for a moment that it would be all too clear that he didn't belong there. Oddly, no one seemed to notice. In fact, the not noticing was so obvious, he could have convinced himself that he'd grown invisible.

He walked back through the hotel and back out to the car. Two of the hotel's uniformed doormen were helping a handsome young couple get their suitcases into the back of a cab.

"We'll wait here awhile," Shanahan said.

"Fine," the driver said.

"Then, my guess is we'll follow some guy in a taxi."

"Cool," the driver said.

Twenty-Four

The wait was about twenty minutes. A couple of cabs and cars had come and gone. No buses. This wasn't a place for busloads of plump, colorfully dressed folks on a beach vacation. This was for the sleek and young, all dressed in black.

Finally, Pritchardt came stumbling out of the front—neither sleek nor dressed in black. A bellboy had opened the door and stood beside Pritchardt, both concerned about Pritchardt's obvious hurry and the lack of conveyance.

Pritchardt was wearing a tan cotton suit—all wrinkled. Probably the one he wore on the plane. If he'd packed at all, he had packed in a hurry and had no doubt planned for a short trip.

"That our guy?" the driver said.

"The one."

If Pritchardt felt some urgency to get where he was going, his cab driver didn't pick up on it or didn't care. The car moved lazily off the drive and onto Collins.

The Towne Car eased forward, nosing out

into the traffic and followed. Shanahan's
driver seemed to be enjoying himself, but
was relaxed about it. Shanahan couldn't
have found a better person for the job. He
stayed behind a few car lengths and even
allowed cars to move in between them.

It was a beautiful day.

"Your guy's heading toward some of the
ritziest areas."

"That's why I wanted a car like this."

"I gotta tell you. If he's going to Star Island
or a few places like it, we're probably not
going to get in."

"Oh?"

"Lots of gated communities here. Real
security. Not your average rent-a-cop at the
gate either."

The cab kept going. Finally, it was obvious
to the driver that the little two-car entourage
was heading for Key Biscayne.

"We might be in luck," the driver said.
"Lots of money. And a lot of it isn't behind
a locked gate."

"Good."

"Then again, some of these folks have
private security."

"That would figure," Shanahan said to
himself, thinking about the thugs. "A little
higher class, isn't it?" Shanahan said. "These
folk don't have to all pitch in for a little
security. They can afford their own, entirely
devoted cops."

"True."

The Towne Car weaved through some fairly ordinary streets and homes that were no more interesting than the upper middle-class homes at Geist in Indianapolis or in Carmel due north of the city.

As the car moved farther in, it was apparent there were homes on the water.

"Richard Nixon lived there," the driver said, pointing. The taxi slowed, but turned and went down a street for which there was a clear warning: *Do not enter.*

The Towne Car eased up just before the sign. Bay Lane and a cross street Shanahan couldn't make out. Pritchardt got out of the taxi, fumbled in his pants, then his wallet for money. He was still nervous. It was obvious by his lack of interest in his surroundings that he was more afraid of where he was going than whether he had been followed. Whatever it was that awaited him was inside a three-story yellow house that occupied a huge chunk of a corner where the street met the ocean.

"Now what, Kimosabe?" the driver asked.

"We'll wait a minute or two and see what happens."

"Man with a plan," the driver said with an upbeat mix of sarcasm and humor.

The driver was having a good time.

The taxi driver, who had apparently been filling out some paperwork, pulled away. He seemed to be in no hurry.

Obviously, Pritchardt wasn't planning on leaving right away.

Shanahan was trying to think about who would have Florida connections. Dickerson said he had a little place in Florida, but came up north in the summer for the grandkids. Could this be the little place? Pritchardt had panicked and made his break shortly after Shanahan talked with Dickerson. Of course, Pritchardt had panicked after Hugh Dart learned of the good doctor's possible involvement.

"You wouldn't happen to know who lives here, would you?" Shanahan asked.

"Why would I know that?"

"You knew where Nixon lived."

The driver laughed. "Well, he doesn't live here anymore."

"True."

The driver picked up the phone. Dialed. "Sharon, please," he said into the phone and waited.

"Hey, Sharon, find out something for me, will you?" The driver gave Sharon the address. There was only a brief wait.

"Jonathan Kelly," the driver said. "Mean anything to you?"

It did not.

"Nope. Anything to you?"

"Yep. Mover, shaker. Big money. Sports, entertainment. Hell, he owns almost everything new and interesting in South Florida. Name is all over the place."

"Puzzle. I don't see the connection," Shanahan said to himself more than the driver.

"Bigger puzzle."

"What?"

"The guy's in hospital. Has been for six months."

"How do you know all of this?"

"In the papers. Constantly. In a coma. Massive heart attack. Probably would have been dead a long time ago if he wasn't so rich. Who knows, maybe he can buy a second life?"

"Can't buy love, but you can buy life," Shanahan said almost involuntarily. "Why is the story playing so big?"

"He's an important guy. Lots of speculation with the will. The old wife. The new wife. The kids. I mean the question of who controls all this guy's holdings is not only gossip but it's got a lot of important people concerned about the outcome. Some people think he hasn't been running the business for quite awhile."

Shanahan could only shake his head. Still, he wasn't able to narrow things down. Now there was a whole new set of circumstances in a whole new part of the country. The case was getting too big. Then again, he had surprised himself by stirring up so much, scaring a few people. Something obviously wasn't right. He was here. He'd investigate a little farther. He had the time and almost enough money. Maureen was having a little vacation. And Shanahan was just too curious for his own good, he thought.

"Hey, there's your guy," the driver said.

He had come from the side gate and stood on the sidewalk. The sun was blazing now. The light was so bright, nothing was unlit. Even from a block away you could see the expression on Pritchardt's face. It was that of a man just thrown out of a bar.

"What do you want to do?"

"Let's ease back and watch. Wait until he can't notice the movement."

They waited until Pritchardt turned and knocked on the door again. If they didn't want him around, then surely they'd call him a taxi, Shanahan thought.

It was a different taxi. Pritchardt walked out to it as it approached and slowed. Suddenly, it made a U-turn and swept back by the Towne Car. It had a fare. Shanahan couldn't make out who.

Perhaps he'd spoiled it, Shanahan thought.

"Let's see if our man wants a ride."

The Towne Car moved up to the sidewalk where Pritchardt stood. Pritchardt came to the car. Not likely he saw anything through the smoked glass. Shanahan opened the door. Pritchardt peered in.

"Want a ride, Augie?"

"Oh my God!" Pritchardt said.

"Get in."

"No!" He said it petulantly, a child whose defiance is based on fear.

"You gonna walk back to the Delano?"

"What is it to you?"

"Sounds like baby talk to me," Shanahan said. "This isn't the kind of conversation I ever expected to have with a doctor, let alone a professor."

Pritchardt was quiet. He hadn't walked away. Maybe his options were as limited as Shanahan guessed.

"That was a dirty trick," Pritchardt said, finally.

"What brought you out here?"

Pritchardt took a couple of deep breaths. His attempts to compose himself were at least superficially successful.

"I don't think you and I have anything to talk about. I could call and have you arrested."

"For what? Offering you a ride?"

"For stalking me."

"Somehow I think you won't. I'm not sure how friendly you want to be with the police. Get in." Shanahan got out of the car and held the door open for Pritchardt. "Wait here."

"I wouldn't go in there," Pritchardt yelled at Shanahan as the detective slammed the door.

"You don't have to. I am."

"Shit," Pritchardt said, closing his eyes.

Shanahan walked toward the house. All was quiet. No wind. No breeze. Even the air had been hushed. He was at the front. He could see nothing through any of the windows. He thought that if he knocked, he would be turned away. His hunch was to go around the side, through the gate Pritchardt used to make his exit.

The path along the side of the house was lined with flowers—white and yellow blooms, luxuriously dense colors that soon gave way to the view of water, and a lot of it—the private dock and the small yacht tied to it. Another turn found a large swimming pool. And a woman standing at one edge of it, a phone in her hand.

When she saw Shanahan, she said something quietly into the phone, pushed a button and set the phone down on a table next to a stack of fluffy white beach towels.

She was striking. Age had removed what little fleshiness there was in her face. The skin was taut on her high cheekbones and tan. Some eyes mask the inner self. Hers locked the door. They were sharp, clear, intelligent and without sentiment.

Barbara Dart wore a yellow-flower print dress, her silvery blond hair tied back the way Grace Kelly used to do it.

"You are persistent, Mr. Shanahan."

"You haven't changed much," he said. He knew so much about her—had looked at the photographs, read the letters—he felt like he knew her.

Her expression, too, was one that suggested the two of them had known each other for years.

She smiled. "Thank you. You don't seem surprised."

"No."

"Have you figured it all out yet?" she asked, the trace of a grin still inhabiting her look.

"Some of it."

"I'd like to offer a little cliché." She stopped as if waiting for permission. Shanahan nodded. "A lot of water has gone under the bridge since then."

"No doubt."

"There was no murder, Mr. Shanahan," she said. "No one died from another's hand."

"No. Probably not."

"We're getting along fine, so far," she said. "Can I get you something to drink?"

"No. Thank you though."

She laughed. "Don't worry. I didn't have time to whip up a batch of poison. So what do you know?"

"Pritchardt got you the body, didn't he?"

"Yes. A Jane Doe, I think they call it. No

one claimed her body. She was without family, apparently. Fitting. A nice match. Before she died she had granted the state permission to use her body for medical research. Augie fudged her body through the system so that she wouldn't be officially missed or traced."

"It's not all harmless. You sent an innocent man to prison for thirty-five years."

"Innocent?" She smiled.

"Innocent of a murder."

"Maybe. Maybe not. I don't know how much you know about Hugh. But there were a few suspect deaths over the years. And he seemed to profit from them. I had every reason to believe I would be next."

"Why?"

"He wanted to be rid of me."

"Why wouldn't he just divorce you?"

"Because I knew about the money, where it was and how he came by it. And he wanted loose. And the only baggage he wanted to carry was the money, and all of it. And if you'll let me string a few more 'ands' together here ... AND he knew he couldn't destroy me as he had done his first wife—turning a shy, trusting girl into a raving lunatic. I was a little too tough for that."

"Pretty tough, still."

She looked at him with those cool eyes as she considered his comment. She smiled, obviously choosing to take his description as a compliment.

"A survivor, Mr. Shanahan. I've come a long way. Again. Even longer. I have a new identity."

"Plenty of money," Shanahan added.

"Yes."

"A powerful standing in the community."

"Yes." She reached toward the stack of towels. "I'm going to have a drink. Why don't you join me?"

"Do I have a choice?"

"Not really." She pulled out a nickel-plated, snub-nosed .38.

Twenty-Five

Shanahan hadn't been too concerned by the turn of events. Outside, in the navy-blue Lincoln sat the driver.

Then again... He felt that sudden, sickening feeling in his stomach—the kind of feeling a guy has hitting an unsuspected dip in the highway.

There was the paunchy, well-tanned man from Maureen's show house. He was at the other end of a long hall, talking with the young Cuban driver.

The tanned man laughed, handed the young driver something too close to the color of money not to be money. The young man nodded. He nodded. Then nodded again. Then once again.

The conversation was in Spanish. The young Cuban wiped his forehead. He nodded.

There was entirely too much nodding for Shanahan. The driver's nervously agreeable nature did not bode well.

Shanahan looked back at Barbara Dart. Barbara was fixing herself the drink she had promised. But in the back doorway now was the tall man with the scarred face. He had taken over possession of the nickel-plated .38 while his boss fiddled with the ice.

Shanahan had outsmarted himself. Maureen didn't know where he'd gone. That was a bad thing. It was also a good thing. Maybe they didn't know where *she* was. Then again, maybe they knew it all. The driver could tell them where he met his client.

"If you were someone else," Barbara Dart said, holding a tall glass of something clear, "I'd just offer you a tidy sum—tidy sum, isn't that quaint?—for you to forget what you know."

"You could still do that," Shanahan said.

"But nothing seems to stop you."

"You haven't really tried money yet." Unfortunately the truth was in his voice.

"Mr. Shanahan, I would never be able to trust you. You are much too honest to be trustworthy."

"Yeah, something to be said for lust, greed, gluttony..."

"There's something to be said for making it through life when every possible obstacle is thrown in your way, Mr. Shanahan. When you get a start like I did, you do things. Is survival one of the seven deadly sins?" She didn't wait for an answer. "A tough world. I don't know what your philosophy is. Mine is to be tougher and smarter than those who would hurt me. And there's a helluva lot of people out there who would hurt me if they could."

Shanahan heard a door shut. The driver, probably. He heard muffled sounds from somewhere else. The dull, muffled sounds of conversation somewhere beyond them.

The taps on the door of Shanahan's room at the Art Deco Hotel and Golf Club were polite—firm but not demanding. The taps were followed by a half minute of silence. Then another half dozen taps. The lack of response brought a voice:

"Important message from Mr. Shanahan."

More quiet. Another series of taps. Then the sound of metal on metal. Scratching.

Howie Cross could see them through the tiny hole. He backed away and into the main room. Then he went into the bathroom, where Maureen was waiting.

"You mind sharing a bath?" he whispered, opening the shower curtain and stepping in.

"Not at the moment," she said. She smiled. A very nervous smile. The lips widened in a grin. "I've always looked forward to dying in a bathtub. It would be nice to have some music and maybe a glass of wine."

"Thanks to Shanahan's invitation, at least you won't be dying alone."

He reached into his jacket pocket and retrieved the roll of quarters he carried and clasped the fingers of his right hand around it.

Being caught in the room with Maureen, without a means of escape and without a weapon wasn't smart. These were two beefy guys. Neither looked friendly. And they were probably packing. No, this wasn't smart. Then again, he thought, he wasn't known for smart moves.

The scratching sounds stopped. In their place came the recognizable clicks. The two goons had unlocked the door.

Maureen and Howie held their breaths. They could see a shadow coming toward the shower curtain. A fat hand appeared on the shower bar and there was an abrupt rip. Just as the curtain flashed open, Howie's right fist bounced high off the heavy-set guy's cheekbone.

It was as if the guy's head was jet-propelled. It launched to the right, body lurching over the sink, head careening against the mirror. The mirror cracked. Howie was out of the tub, grabbing the guy's head. Then, using the guy's skull like a shot-putter, he heaved it, and the glass in the mirror cracked forming a spider-web pattern splattered with red.

Maureen had retrieved the man's pistol and was about to level her aim at the other heavy-set guy coming through the doorway in the bathroom, when Howie flung the door at him, then opened it. By the time the guy focused on the two intended victims, Maureen had the gun steady.

"Hi," she said cheerfully. "I wondered when we'd see each other again."

Howie took the guy's pistol.

"Yeah," the guy said. He nodded toward Howie. "I see you got yourself another dog."

The guy seemed a little dazed. He was feeling his forehead to see if was all still there when Howie's quarter-roll-clenching fist came down on the guy's nose and mouth. He rolled back, but didn't go down.

"I'm a pretty even-tempered guy," Howie said, taking the second gun. "So I thought you wouldn't mind if I got even."

"Hey, it's a job," the guy said.

"Wanna play some golf?" Howie asked.

"What?"

"We got a foursome here," he said, walking over to the semiconscious body on the floor. "Gotta go, fella. A little exercise. A little Florida Sunshine."

Shanahan didn't wonder what they were waiting for. There was obviously some sort of party planned—with Shanahan and Maureen. Maybe Cross. Cross was due in.

Pritchardt had joined the group in the kitchen. The pudgy guy with the tan was somewhere else in the house. And there were voices. Whose, Shanahan couldn't make out.

But Pritchardt didn't look happy. He had the look of a scared kid waiting in the principal's office. He was sweating. His eyes stayed on the floor, taking only an occasional furtive look at Barbara Dart and the craggy-faced guy with the scar.

"Kidnapping is a serious offense," Shanahan said. "I'd be willing to look the other way. No harm done yet."

She smiled.

"You may be honest, but you're not that naive."

"You said yourself you hadn't killed anyone."

"That was then," she said calmly.

"Why spoil it?"

"Come on." She shook her head. Wasn't it obvious?

"Husband in a coma. A fortune hanging in the balance. He's worth a lot," Shanahan volunteered.

"A lot?" She laughed. "This isn't Hugh Dart and chump change. This thing comes out, I don't stand a chance against his family in the courts. Hell, I'm not even married to the guy if the truth comes out. I'm still married to Hugh. Isn't that something? I get nada. I'm too old to shake my bootie for some other old codger."

Shanahan didn't say anything. She had done well for herself. Money. Power. She was still beautiful as well. Shanahan thought that the evil in people did eventually show up in their faces. If that were true, Barbara Dart had kept nature under pretty tight control as well. Her face did show a little hardness for those who looked closely.

"What about you, Mr. Shanahan? You willing to provide me all of this? Keep me in the style to which I've become so accustomed."

"And what about Hugh?" Shanahan asked.

"Hugh?"

"A financial arrangement, Deets," Hugh Dart said, coming in around the corner, behind the craggy-faced bodyguard.

"Oh," Shanahan said.

"You don't say that like you're completely surprised," Hugh said.

"No. Not completely. I saw a scam. I just didn't know exactly how all the pieces fit."

"She's got me by the balls as usual," Dart said. "But the feeling isn't all that unpleasant. I keep getting money as long as I keep shutting up. More than I had initially. More than I would get if I blabbed." There was a long silence. "I'm sorry, Deets. I tried to get you off the case. I do admire you."

"Maybe you'll carve something nice on my headstone."

"Yeah," he said with a half smile and a shrug.

"How'd you know where to find her?" Shanahan asked Hugh Dart.

"I called him," she said.

"You were getting too close," Hugh Dart said. "And you wouldn't be scared off, or fired, apparently. You were like that little rabbit."

"Were," Shanahan said.

Dart shrugged again. It was obvious he didn't like what was about to happen. But when push came to shove, it would be Hugh Dart doing the pushing. "She wanted to make a deal. Cheaper to buy me off than do something drastic and risk all of this." He gestured toward the grand house. "And this is just a teensy weensy little bit of what she has."

"And now?"

Hugh Dart looked away. "I'm sorry. I really am."

"Others know," Shanahan said, then regretted saying so.

"It will all be taken care of," she said.

"Dickerson involved in all this too?"

"What makes you say that?" Barbara asked, seemingly more amused than concerned.

"Pritchardt's way too squeamish to get involved in something like this without a lot of prodding, hand-holding and someone to actually do the dirty work. He's a big baby."

Barbara Dart shrugged.

Pritchardt looked up from the spot he was staring at on the floor.

"A controllable baby, most of the time,"

she said.

That seemed to make him angry, but he didn't bite. Just turned his eyes to the floor again.

"This time he's going to be an accessory to a real murder," Shanahan said. Another long silence. "Oh, I see. There's going to be a big boating accident, isn't there?"

Pritchardt looked up again. "What?"

"Don't pee in your pants, Augustus," Barbara Dart said. "He's trying to get you upset."

"Why not? You're a wimp, Pritchardt. You gave her away once. You think she's going to trust you now? This is big time. Two for the price of one. Maybe you were a hero. You jumped in to save me. And there were sharks..."

Pritchardt stood up. It looked for a moment like he was going to say or possibly even do something.

"Sit down," she said, not bothering to look at him. "He's got something to lose. He'll behave."

"Augie wouldn't do well in prison," Hugh Dart said. "Right, Augie? He'll mind his manners."

"And you, Hugh? Why do you feel so secure?"

"I didn't come all this way without a little insurance. I don't get burned twice by the same ... person." He grinned. "Mrs. Jonathan Kelly is much too big to hide these days. It's all written down, ready to be released if I don't make regular contact. If I go bye bye, she's thrown to the sharks too. Inquiring minds will want to know."

"You're not angry at all? All is forgiven?" Shanahan asked. "Thirty-five years and you don't mind?"

"Yeah, I'd love to make her life miserable for the next thirty-five years. But, kill the golden goose? I'm mad, not crazy."

"You were betrayed."

"It's not working, Deets. You have to care a lot about a person to feel betrayed by them." Hugh looked at Barbara. Her face was made of stone. "Double-crossed, but not betrayed. I don't give a shit about anybody involved in this ... Pritchardt or," Dart continued, looking at Barbara, "this one. Though I have to admit, you weathered the years pretty good." He looked back to Shanahan. "She won. Good for her. I don't like the idea a woman beats me, but..."

"Money heals all wounds," she said.

"Yes, who knows what might happen? Mr. Kelly is not in good health," Hugh said, smiling. "Barbara Kelly, after a normal period of grief, might want to marry again."

Her stone face showed signs of cracking.

"She and I, well, we both have a lot in common."

273

Twenty-Six

"I'd like to see you guys undress," Cross said.

"What?" said the guy who had just staggered to consciousness.

"Take your clothes off. Get naked."

Maureen grinned. She held the gun steady.

"What's with you guys from Indiana?" the other guy said.

"We're all a little repressed," Cross said. "You know how that goes? Bible Belt. Then we get out of town. All hell breaks loose. Strip."

They didn't budge.

"I can help," Cross said. "You want me to help?"

"No," the larger of the two said. He began taking his clothes off.

"Does she have to be here?" the other guy said.

"You're worried about *her*?"

They undressed.

Cross grinned. "I don't know. You guys ever heard of a gym? I always thought mob hit men would be in pretty good shape.

Wouldn't you think so, Maureen?"

"Just can't get good help these days."

"All right, leave your clothes here and let's go!" Cross said.

"What? Where?"

"We're gonna go to the golf course. Won't that be fun?"

Maureen looked puzzled.

"This is the Art Deco Hotel and Golf Club," he said to her.

"What are we doing in here?" Hugh Dart asked. "I've spent most of my life inside. This is Florida. You have a pool. Come on, Augie, Barbara." He looked at the tall skinny guy with the scar and the craggy face. "And whoever you are. You look like you could use some sun."

The craggy-faced guy didn't move, didn't blink.

"Why not?" Barbara said. "I'm getting a little tired of the kitchen. And I don't want the rest of the house messed up."

"She was a neat wife," Hugh said to Shanahan. "Come on, Deets. Get a moment or two of Florida retirement."

"She was watching you from the moment you got out, wasn't she?"

"Yeah. I knew she would. She knew when I was getting out, knew I'd get in touch with my mother and my daughter. She knew Melanie was seeing a private eye. I would have told you all this, but you didn't believe she was still alive."

Hugh smiled. "Life's funny, isn't it?"

"Yeah. Hilarious."

The attractive woman at the hotel desk looked at the two naked men moving into and across the small lobby. Guided by Cross, they went up the steps.

"I've called the police," the woman said calmly, conversation directed at Maureen.

"Nudists!" Maureen said in a tone of mock exasperation.

Up a dark stairway to the roof—a third-floor, outdoor miniature golf course. In disrepair. The innards, the underground pipes that directed the routes of the golf balls, were laid bare and rusty. The larger-than-life clowns with gaping mouths looked as if they'd had lobotomies and the human-sized mice were all dressed up with no place to go.

"Have fun boys," Cross said.

He and Maureen descended the stairs, letting the huge fire door to the roof close, eliminating access back into the hotel.

"Golf club, now it makes sense," Maureen said. "How'd you know it was up there?"

"I always case a place before I get comfortable. This one didn't take long. Hi," he said to the woman at the desk. "I think they're playing a couple of rounds of golf. God knows what they're using for balls."

276

The elevator dropped them to the walkway. In seconds they were amidst the crowd on the sidewalk.

"We'll take their car," Howie said.

"Which one is it?"

"Well," Howie said, "let's see." He pulled out a key chain, pressed a little leather tab and heard the beep and the lights flashed on.

"Magic," Howie Cross said. The car that beeped was a gray Mercedes. Not the big expensive one. But not the new little $50,000 "economy" model either.

The police pulled up, double-parked in front of the Art Deco Hotel and Golf Club.

"Should we be in their car?" Maureen asked. "Won't they—"

"I think they'll be very quiet for awhile," Cross interrupted. "But we should move pretty quick. You said Shanahan rented a limo. You remember what service he used?"

Shanahan chose the sun. A pure white Adirondack sitting on a manicured green lawn between the pool and the water. The prospect of death had chilled his bones. Behind him, he could hear music—bossa nova.

Before settling in, he glanced back. Barbara was on the phone. Hugh Dart was standing in the shade, nursing a glass that contained something the color of whiskey. The craggy-faced man with the scars stood

277

only a few feet from Shanahan. In his narrow-lapeled suit and thin tie, he looked like a syndicate accountant. An armed syndicate accountant. He still had the .38.

Shanahan settled back into the chair, took a deep breath. The full force of the sun was on his face and arms. It felt good. A hint of salt was in the air.

For a moment, all his thoughts were with Maureen. He hoped Cross had made the flight. Shanahan paid for the tickets, the room. Cross had promised.

Shanahan looked up. His father was standing there—lean, young and shirtless. He was digging a post hole. A new letter box laid near the pile of earth to one side. The elder Shanahan looked up as young Dietrich approached. The father smiled.

"Give the old man a hand, hmmmmn?"

Shanahan felt queasy, lightheaded. Faint. He felt as if he were sinking. He shook himself, ripped himself from his father's grasp. He had to keep his mind on Maureen.

The yacht bobbed lightly in the water. "Desafinado," was its name. Stan Getz, Shanahan thought. He felt better. His bones were warming. Not at all unpleasant given the circumstances.

"They should be here by now," Shanahan heard Barbara Dart say. Anxiety was in her voice. The tanned man reassured her. She wasn't happy with his optimism.

The craggy-faced man with the scars stood quietly. He stood in the sun, in his suit, tie pulled tight up against the starched collar. He stood watch over Shanahan. He wasn't even perspiring.

Shanahan looked around again, searching for something or someone to hang a hope upon. Nothing. Would they dare shoot him? Logic would tell him that he could run for it. They wouldn't chance a murder on the grounds. Like most people, Shanahan decided to wait for a more sure opportunity, despite the fact he was sure there was none. No escape.

The quick but vivid visit with his father. The dark angel standing guard. Away from everyone. The endless ocean. It all seemed like death to him.

What Cross and Maureen found out at the limo office was that the driver was still out, presumably with Shanahan. The man in the office who spoke English with a heavy Spanish accent said that the car had been booked from 10 to 2. It was now only 12:30.

"Can you call him?" Cross asked the man who was fingering a small gold chain that disappeared into the white cotton, short-sleeved dress shirt. It was a small office. Two women worked at plain gray desks—the utilitarian kind that banks used in the fifties and sixties before they all became colonial

279

living rooms.

"Ches," the man said. He consulted a small spiral-bound notebook, then punched in the numbers. His eyes kept drifting to Maureen, who looked better in her white cotton, short-sleeved dress shirt.

"No answer," the man said.

"Will he call in?" Maureen asked.

"Maybe." He shrugged.

"You talking about Hector?" a woman asked. "He call, you know?"

"He did? What did he say?" Maureen asked.

"He want me to look up who live at some address."

"You still have the address?" Cross asked.

"Yes," she said. She leaned over, pulled a waste basket from beneath the desk. She reached in, finding a crumpled piece of paper. She read off the address as Cross wrote it down.

Key Biscayne. Cross knew Miami about as well as he knew Tibet. He paid $20 for a used Miami area street directory, and the two of them were back out on the hot concrete, climbing into the gray Mercedes.

"At least we've got an address," Cross said.

"You figure we're all right in this car?"

"I don't know. If the two goons are taken away by the cops, they might not even know their car is gone. Even if they do, I don't know how much they'll say to the police. I'm

280

not sure how much talking they'll want to do to anyone. But if they get to make a call, they might call the very place we're going. Then again, with all the police bureaucracy, they might not get to make a call for hours..."

"What are you saying, Howie?"

"I have absolutely no idea."

"What do we do?"

"I have absolutely no idea."

"Make up something."

"All right, let's assume the fates are on our side. We go here," he said, waving the piece of paper. "As quickly as we can. I don't want them planning a welcome." He looked through the street directory trying to match the address he had written on a corner of a napkin to a street on the map in the book. "This is the address." He put his finger on the spot, then handed the book to Maureen.

"I'm navigating, I take it." She looked more closely. "Right on the ... ocean," she said as if the word "ocean" bore so much weight she could barely say it. "The edge."

"Has to be a good neighborhood," he said. "No bad houses on the water."

To get to the limo office, they had traversed the MacArthur Causeway. Now they were crossing the water again, over the long Rickenbacker Causeway, over Biscayne Bay. The pale gray Mercedes moved smoothly over the pale gray concrete bridge. The

Miami skyline was behind them. On land again, they drove through what appeared to be a well-kept park.

Then into neighborhoods. The approach to the neighborhood was deceiving. Nice homes, but nothing to prepare them for what sat on the edges of the Key itself.

"We're close," she said. "A left up here."

"OK," he said quietly, as if anyone could hear them. He pulled the Mercedes to the side.

"It's a short street," she said. "The ocean can't be more than a few feet behind these houses."

"Wait then," he said, undoing his safety belt.

"Where are you going?"

"Just to take a look. I won't do anything, I promise. Just a look and I'll be right back."

The phone rang.

It startled both of them.

"Don't answer it," Cross said.

"OK."

He got out of the car, walked down the street. She watched, listening to the constant electronic beep of the phone. He crossed the street the house had to be on, looked down. He went to the other side, paused a moment, then returned.

"Now what do we do?" she asked when he opened the door.

"I think I know. Odd, isn't it?" He scooted

in, put the car in gear, then backed up nearly half a block. Then he pulled forward, into a drive.

"You know these people?" she asked.

"My Aunt Sylvia."

"What are we doing?"

"I don't think anyone's here," he said.

"What makes you think that?"

"There's a FedEx tag on the door. An attempted delivery."

"So they're not home—then what, smarty pants?"

"We get to see the back. My guess is both houses have access to the beach." He got out of the car. She followed. "Wait here."

"No way."

"Then, stay as far away from the house as you can. They may have an alarm that goes off with movement."

They heard the phone begin to beep again just before they silenced the sound by closing the doors to the car.

Shanahan felt strangely at peace. He worried about Maureen. But there was nothing he could do at the moment. The yacht bobbed and tilted ever so slightly.

He could hear voices behind him. Barbara's especially.

"They're not picking up," she said. "Where in the hell are they?"

Twenty-Seven

"A kid and his dog," Cross said, once he was at the back of the house. "Isn't that wonderful?"

"What?"

"Over there." Cross pointed to a young boy, maybe ten years old, on the beach with what appeared to be a Black Lab.

"OK? What?"

"Cover."

"Cover."

"You, me, the kid and the dog. The great American family walking along the water's edge, down there." He nodded in the other direction.

"That the house?"

"Yeah. People outside. I can see their heads."

"A boat."

"A yacht."

"OK, a floating device. We don't want to put some kid in danger."

"We won't." He looked back at the house. It was striking. From the front it wasn't any more special than the homes on Meridian in

284

Indianapolis. But with a view of the side and back of the home, you could tack on a few million in improvements, plus the ocean.

"Go get Timmy and Lassie, OK?" Cross said. He took off his shirt, left it on the lawn. He took off his shoes.

"This isn't a nude beach, is it?"

"Not nude. Casual. We live here, remember."

The two of them took a left to where the kid was playing, before heading right, to the big yellow house.

"What's the dog's name?" Cross asked the kid.

"Boomer."

"Boomer. Good name."

"Who lives down there in the big yellow house?"

"Mr. Kelly. What are you doing at the Carrolls'?"

"House-sitting. This is my lovely wife, Maureen."

"Hi," the kid said, tossing the tennis ball up in the air and catching it.

"Hi. And you are?"

"Jason."

"Jason. Jason and Boomer," Cross said, snatching the ball midair.

"Boomer fetches?" Cross asked.

"He's the best," the kid said.

"OK." Cross cocked his arm and threw the ball. It arched over two lawns, hit the pebbles and angled within two houses of the sloping yard at the big yellow house.

The dog had taken off as soon as the ball was launched, checking the trajectory and almost running under it.

"Let's go, Jason," Cross said. The three of them walked down toward the ball. "He's good."

"I told you," Jason said.

The dog came rushing back, bringing the ball to Jason.

"Give me a couple more shots, OK?" Cross asked.

"Sure."

"You know the people who live in the big yellow house?"

"Not much. I've seen them a couple of times. Going to the boat."

"See," Maureen said.

"They know your parents?"

"I don't think so. Mr. Kelly is pretty important. Except Dad says he's pretty sick. He says the guy might die or something."

"Bet he wishes for 'or something,'" Cross said. He tossed the ball and watched the sleek Black Lab head back down to the water's edge, as he, Maureen and the kid headed closer to the big yellow house.

For a moment Shanahan thought he was having hallucinations again—if that's what those all too vivid images were. He saw Maureen first, her auburn hair glinting even redder in the strong Florida sun. Then he realized it was Cross who walked just behind her, glancing up at the house. Cross's eyes met Shanahan's. This was the extent of the acknowledgment.

The dark angel and Barbara Dart's tanned mouthpiece would recognize Maureen if they saw her. Then again, the little family they had created was a perfect cover. What next, though? At least three of Barbara Dart's minions were armed.

Shanahan heard Mrs. Kelly's name being called. She was standing next to the dark angel when Shanahan turned to look.

The tanned man was standing in the doorway that led out to the pool.

"Phone!" he yelled.

"Get those people to leave," she told the craggy-faced dark angel. She went back to the table for the phone as her messenger descended the shallow slope, down to the trespassers.

"You will have to leave," the craggy-faced man said, moving close to Cross, who dropped his sunglasses, then dropped down as if to retrieve them.

"I'm sorry, what?"

"This is private property. I'm afraid you will have to leave."

Cross pulled the 9 mm he'd taken from the previous goons from the waistband of his trousers and pressed the barrel against the messenger's crotch.

"Here, I've shown you mine, now you show me yours. Only I want to see the handle first, OK?"

"Jason," Maureen said to the boy, "you need to go home now." She tossed the tennis ball so boy and dog would act quickly on her request.

Cross looked up to see the look on Mrs. Dart's face. Whatever she heard on her little cellular phone was added to her intuitive feelings about Cross and his little family.

Cross moved behind the craggy-faced man and, as he passed Shanahan, tossed the nickel-plated .38 he'd retrieved onto Shanahan's chair.

Shanahan stood, looked down the slope toward Maureen. She too was holding a pistol. The child and his dog were walking away slowly. The kid's mouth was agape. All of this had gone too far. He felt the sun beating down on him. The light was starkly brutal. Barbara Dart Kelly slowly put the phone down.

The slightly pudgy tanned man came out from the house. He paused at the strange gathering of souls near the pool.

"The keys to the boat," she said, snapping her fingers at the tanned pudgy guy.

He looked around, trying hard to figure out what was going on, but knowing better than to disobey Mrs. Kelly.

"You're not going to kill me," she said, glancing first at Cross, then at Shanahan. She smiled.

The tanned pudgy man dropped the keys in Mrs. Dart's hand. She started walking down the slope to the small pier.

"I'd have killed you, you know," she said to Shanahan.

"I believe you would, Mrs. Dart."

"Then we understand each other."

"We do."

She walked up the pier and onto the yacht. No one moved. Everyone waited, staring at the million-dollar boat. She disappeared inside it.

Soon there was the deep rumble of the engines.

"How far do you think she'll get?" Cross asked.

"Who knows. She's probably got a stash buried somewhere," Shanahan said.

Cross nodded. "Maybe she's got nine lives. Think she'll have a good time?"

"I think so," Shanahan said.

Maureen moved toward Shanahan. "That's about the third smile I've ever seen on your face, Mr. Shanahan."

Shanahan noticed that the remaining souls, thugs included, stood staring out to sea, the yacht sending back rolls of watery exhaust. Suddenly a man appeared on the rear of the boat. Hugh Dart and the American flag waved back at them.

"I can't think of a more lovely couple," Shanahan said. "They certainly deserve each other."

"You guys better get your résumés in shape," Cross told the guy with the tan and the dark angel. "She's not coming back. And there will be a lot of hell to pay. You might tell the twins as well."

"Who was that guy, anyway?" the sun-tanned man asked with the stunned look of disbelief.

"That..." Cross paused for a moment, "was the Lone Ranger."

"That," Shanahan said, "was Mrs. Kelly's husband."

"One of them," Maureen said.

"I'm certainly glad I got to share this leg of the flight with you," Cross said to the man in the seat next to him. He got no response. "So, Augie, how are you feeling?" No response. "You know you're in line for that job with Doctor Frankenstein. Anybody tell you you're a damned fine body snatcher?"

"You are a son of a bitch."

"I know. I've had a bad attitude all my life. No respect for authority. And here you are. A doctor. A professor. Above reproach."

"No reason to be so smug. Nothing is going to happen. It happened thirty-five years ago. There is a statute of limitation.

And I had nothing to do with your friend's kidnapping."

"You had me beat up pretty bad," Howie said.

"Wasn't me. It was Dickerson. Radiquet said you called him asking about Dart and his daughter. You asked too many questions."

"Nobody's gonna burn for this one, it looks like," Howie said. "Everybody lives happily ever after, right?"

Augie wouldn't speak.

The Lincoln Road Mall isn't a mall in the usual sense. It's an open space in South Beach that runs several blocks, lined on either side of the broad landscaped walkway with interesting shops, lively clubs and exotic restaurants.

It was a warm clear night. There was considerable bustle. Roller-bladers, lovers, loafers, revelers, diners.

Maureen was on her second glass of wine, and Shanahan had ventured into the world of microbreweries.

"Don't tell Harry."

"He'd think it was an affectation, right?"

"I think drinking wheat beer is worse than drinking daiquiris."

"So you're done, huh?" she asked as the waiter brought the grilled swordfish. "With all of this?"

"Almost."

On the way back to the hotel room, the two of them took a starlit detour to the beach.

Revelry was just beginning where the neon glowed and the babble of foreign tongues planned evenings that would extend well beyond Shanahan's consciousness.

Even so, he felt he had made it through another dangerous twist in the road. Time now was a gift that he treasured rather than endured. And it was Maureen's doing.

She had introduced him to so many things —not the least of which was the importance of taking risks.

He took her hand.

"There's a ship out there," she said. "Do you see it?"

"Too dark, Maureen. Can't see a thing but you."

"Well, there is. I see it, slinking through the darkness."

Twenty-Eight

"Well," Howie asked. "How much do you want to know?" He and Melanie sat by the window at Amici's in Indianapolis. The waiter had brought the bread earlier and the Chianti. He now set the salads in front of them.

Melanie looked out, presumably at the quaint turn-of-the-century homes across Michigan Street. These were the homes that fronted the southern side of Lockerbie, where one of the city's oldest neighborhoods had been preserved.

"You want to go for a walk later?" she asked.

"That'd be great," Howie said. He took the question as his answer and he told himself not to spoil it. He also told himself that if she couldn't face her past, she'd have a helluva time with the future. And the funny thing was, he was beginning to be interested in her future.

They didn't talk much during dinner. But the emotional distance between them didn't seem all that far.

Outside, a slight chill, a faint reminder of winter was resident in the breeze as they walked on the brick street. If one could erase the automobiles, it wouldn't be difficult to imagine an earlier era, a less complicated time, perhaps.

"All right," she said.

"All right?"

"Tell me. Tell me what you found out. Let's get this over with."

"Well, I don't know how you'll take this, but Barbara is alive."

Melanie laughed. It wasn't broad and encompassing, but ironic, almost bitter.

"I suppose that's good news ... for her anyway."

"It's not really news to her," Howie said, immediately regretting the constant and often involuntary imposition of his smart-alecky nature.

She laughed again. This time without an edge. "I suppose that's true."

"I'm an absolute genius when it comes to stating the obvious. I'm sorry."

"And where is she? Florida?"

"Actually, I don't know. She's run off again."

"She has?" Melanie said, grinning.

"With your father."

Her smile vanished. They had gone two blocks before she spoke again. "Makes you wonder, doesn't it?"

"I guess."

She stopped, stood at the corner, under a gaslight.

"I mean I can see the humor here," she said. "Really. But what does that say for me?" Then she caught herself. "I really do hate self-pity. Let's go do something."

"What?"

"Anything. Something different."

Back at home, Shanahan slid into the morning routine. He fed the cat, let the dog out in the backyard, ground the coffee and picked up the morning paper.

He thought there ought to be some headline about it all. "Murder Victim Alive. Innocent Man Spends 35 Years in Prison."

He wasn't sure that headline or anything like it would ever see the top of a doorstep. But he figured there were some folks who ought to know about it. He'd give Dickerson until 10 this morning. Then Shanahan would give him a call.

"Hello, Mr. Dickerson?"

"Yes?"

"Shanahan."

"What is it that you want? Don't you think we should quit playing this little game?"

"That's what I'm calling about. I thought maybe Pritchardt might have told you."

"What?"

"We found Barbara Dart."

There was a long pause.

"You what?"

"We found Barbara Dart." Shanahan wasn't sure what was so surprising. That she was alive or that she had been found.

"Congratulations then. But let me tell you something, this is all history to me in any event. Of no concern."

"Well, maybe you'll appreciate the humor in it anyway. She got away again. With Hugh. My guess is she has access to some big dollars somewhere."

"When did she leave?"

"Day before yesterday."

"Really?" Again Shanahan couldn't determine his tone—surprise, fear, gladness. Could be any of them.

"Like you said, that's all history. Though I did notice, just back and looking at the brochure of the company you're president of ... that a Mrs. Jonathan Kelly is the CEO. I'd have never guessed that was her ... you know, when I read it before."

Shanahan heard a click. Then a dial tone.

"You gave her time to get away," Maureen said, coming up to his chair.

"Everybody's got to pay somehow. Pritchardt couldn't have done this without someone a whole lot stronger behind him. My guess is that she paid both of them off through the company. Had them both set for life. Her too."

"Pritchardt's money too?"

"Yep."

"Anybody else on the list we'd recognize?"

"I looked. No one."

"Then it's over."

"Maybe."

Twenty-Nine

"Thought I'd stop by," Shanahan said to John G. Radiquet.

"Yes?" He turned his head. The "yes" was an acknowledgment of Shanahan's presence, not a welcome. "You were just in the neighborhood, I take it?"

"I thought you might be curious."

"Curiosity is for the young. When you get my age..." He turned his body in the seat to get a better look. His eyes showed some recognition. "Well, you are my age aren't you? I'm not used to talking to people of my generation anymore. And the odd thing is you are curious. So another theory bites the dust."

His words were thick. It was the port. Two in the afternoon and Radiquet had imbibed more than a bit. He hadn't bothered to hide the glass or the bottle, which was two-thirds gone.

"Curiosity is for the young, you say?"

"You are a young man, Mr. Shanahan. Look at you. Moving about. Interested in life. Still solving puzzles. You've solved one, haven't you?"

"Maybe."

"The secret of life? What happens when you die?"

"A little smaller mystery, maybe."

"Thank goodness. I wasn't sure I wanted to know the answers to those questions, which of course plays to my failed thesis that curiosity is not always a good thing. What surprise is it to which you treat this unsuspecting mind?"

"I'm not sure that any of this will come as a surprise."

Radiquet smiled. "Have a seat?"

Shanahan sat in one of the high-backed chairs in front of Radiquet's desk, back to the windows that looked out upon the Circle.

"Barbara Dart is alive."

There was no change in Radiquet's expression. Even mildly drunk, the lawyer was still a lawyer.

Shanahan continued. "August Pritchardt had procured the body to stand in for her in death."

Still no reaction. He seemed relaxed.

"My guess is that Dickerson helped her a great deal. Probably shored up Pritchardt's less than robust psyche, probably hauled the body and, more than anything else, helped set up the system to launder the cash. How am I doing?"

Radiquet didn't react to the question. He seemed lost in thought. Then his body jerked, as if he'd just been startled, suddenly awakened.

He shook his head, exhaled. "Glass of port?"

"That'd be nice."

Radiquet didn't have to get up. He reached into the cabinet beside his desk and brought out another glass. He poured the glass a little more than half full, reached forward to set it on the far side of the desk, within Shanahan's reach.

"Cigar?"

"No, thank you."

"She was brilliant," Radiquet said. Admiration was apparent on his face. "Pritchardt had been accused of ... let's just say that one of his students accused him of some ... had observed some ... uh, indelicate behavior. He was up for charges. Barbara was his alibi. She had him by the balls. He was also in awe of her. He had a kind of slave mentality in a way. No matter how much he accomplished in life, he regarded himself as inferior, unworthy, you might say. She recognized that immediately. He might even have helped her without the charges. It was the way their personalities worked together. He was capable of being loyal no matter how he was treated."

Shanahan said nothing while Radiquet got

his breath.

"And I suspect, though I don't know for sure, that Pritchardt wanted Hugh out of the way for other reasons."

"Having to do with money, I bet."

"You win. Hugh was blackmailing Pritchardt, getting him to funnel money from the state's hospital system into various accounts that Hugh had access to. Putting Hugh away would have been appealing to any number of people."

"Dickerson?"

"Quite right. He is a much simpler case. Dickerson needed the money. Desperate. His dealership was going down the tubes. They kept thinking this new model and that would save Studebaker, but it didn't. And the land the dealership was sitting on was losing value—at least at the time. Fact was he was about to lose his mortgage anyway. She knew it. She knew it through Hugh, who was pressing Dickerson for campaign contributions. Actually, he kept pressing. You can figure where some of those contributions actually went? Dart was burning him."

"And you?"

"And me." He poured himself more of the deep-red port. He looked at it for a moment, shook his head. "The most foolish of all."

"Love."

"Love. I could have been starving and I wouldn't have done it for food. I wouldn't have done it to save my reputation. I wouldn't have done it for anything I could imagine. But her. I never met anyone so ... exquisite. She was beautiful, brilliant."

"Cold."

"Antarctic." Radiquet smiled. "Layers and layers and layers of ice. Brilliant. Beautiful. And oddly fragile. Is she still beautiful?"

"Yes," Shanahan said. "And possibly brilliant. I might have a problem with fragile."

Radiquet had already moved on. "I couldn't say 'no.' How ludicrous it seems now. I was so smart. 'Brilliant,' was a word they used to describe me. I guess I was."

"You guided the jury to come up with a verdict against your own client, all the while they thought you were valiantly fighting for him?"

"I was even credited—can you imagine that—credited for creating a brilliant defense—there's that word again. Brilliant. Word of the day. Anyway I was credited for keeping him out of the electric chair."

"Home free."

"Home free," he said. "Clients were lined up. She vanished. And the funny thing is, I actually got over her. Sort of came to my senses. The only problem was that I had to spend the rest of my life with me." He took a deep drink. The port dribbled. He grabbed his handkerchief, dabbed his lips; but he missed one trail of red, that dripped off his chin onto the white cotton of his shirt.

"It's a strange thing, Mr. Shanahan. I don't drink so much out of remorse, just to deaden things. Maintain a state of unawareness, as my wife said. Then you came along."

"You kept the scrapbook."

He smiled. "Oh no. No. My secretaries did. In those days we kept all of our clippings. The way that particular story was written about in the press was a reconstruction of the past that I would have enjoyed believing. No. The past is not pleasant. Looking ahead seems pretty dismal, if you ask me. And I'm not particularly comfortable in the present, present company excepted, of course."

Shanahan downed what port was left in his glass. He thought it was a bit too sweet. He stood.

"Now what?" Radiquet asked.

"I don't know," Shanahan said. He hadn't thought about it.

Radiquet started laughing. His roly-poly body shaking like gelatin. It was a broad but not necessarily joyous laugh.

The drive back home would be short. Once he got out of the parking garage, the trip east on Washington Street would take no more than ten minutes.

The front of the car dropped down too far as it entered the street and scraped the concrete. No harm done, Shanahan thought.

But the bump jarred something and static now came from the car radio which hadn't worked in at least a decade.

Shanahan pushed one of the buttons. The sound was crystal clear.

He recognized the song. "Desafinado." It had been playing on the beach.

They all got away. But, in the end, had any of them escaped? Whatever you do, or whatever you don't do, stays with you in some way for at least as long as you inhabit the earth.

Maureen was out on the front lawn, kneeling down beside the lawnmower as Shanahan's green Malibu pulled into the driveway. She waved.

It all seemed so real. As real as his brief flashbacks. Perhaps it was the light. He waved back. Sat for a moment in the car, watching her.

He'd come so close to shutting her out when they first met. He hadn't wanted any complications in his life. One moment, even one word, would have changed everything. He very likely would have spent the remainder of his life sitting around, reading old magazines in death's waiting room.

She looked up again, smiled.

The music played.